PRAISE FOR DUVAY KNOX

The Pussy Detective is the best novel I have read in the past five years! It feels like James Joyce wrote Blaxploitation and left his pretense at home. It's fun, surreal, and kept my attention from cover to cover. This book is THE underground novel of the year.

— DANIEL W. WRIGHT, AUTHOR OF *LOVE LETTERS FROM THE UNDERGROUND*

This book takes chances in more than one way, and it all pays off through a unique narrative. The greatest part of *The Pussy Detective* is its heart, and there's a hell of a lot of it!

— PATRICK R. MCDONOUGH, HOST OF DEAD HEADSPACE PODCAST

A new kind of original writing that grabs your attention with its perfect balance of black erotica, occult mystery & spiritual enlightenment.

— ANDREA MCCAY

DuVay Knox has invented a new genre of Blaxploitation Bizarro that's absurdly poignant and utterly refreshing. Naughty, edgy, and utterly hilarious I read this one to the end in one sitting.

— JERRY DRAKE, AUTHOR OF *HAZEL DREW WAS A GOOD GIRL: SLEUTHING THE MURDER THAT INSPIRED TWIN PEAKS* (FORTHCOMING FROM CLASH BOOKS)

T0098884

THE PUSSY DETECTIVE

DUVAY KNOX

CL◢SH

I dedicate this work to my 2 Biggest Fans:

DENISE KNOX and COCO LOTUS. They never let me forget that I could write something folks would wanna read if I really put my mind to it. And without them this book would not have been possible.

I also wanna shout out mah Mama & Daddy becuz if they had not got 2getha to have me I would not even be around to have life to say a few werds that became this book.

A HOODOO PRIEST NAMED REVEREND DADDY HOODOO OPENS UP AN OCCULT DETECTIVE AGENCY TO HELP FIND LOST & MISSING PUSSIES

1

You probably wondering how I got into Finding Lost Pussy.

Well, actually, I was born to do this.

Everybody cums here with certain sets of Skills that only THEY kan do.

Finding Lost or Missing Pussy is mines.

Technically speaking, finding the SPIRIT or ESSENCE of Da Pussy is whats actually being done.

The Woman who Suffers with this treacherous, vengeful condition is known as a Cold Maid.

She dies inside.

Some women go krazy — or even silent, refusing to speak ever again.

Some OFF themselves.

They most sertainly never make love again.

You see, every living thing has a Spirit that dwells within it.

Even Furniture.

Its alive, too.

In fact, everything that exists in this 4th Dimensional construct that we live in is alive (Yes, 4 Dimensions as science fails to realize...more about that later).

Even though we mite not think of it as such.

So when a Pussy goes MISSING or is LOST what we mean in this bizness is that its Spirit has left the dwelling of the PUSSY PROPER.

This is called LOST PUSSY or MISSING PUSSY.

And Im one of the best and last in the world who is an expert in the ancient art of Finding Lost or Missing Pussy.

———

Here is what happens: One day a woman wakes up and the Spiritual Essence that lives within her Honey Pot is gone like a fart in a dust storm!

Its often sum devastating shit.

What woman wants to live a life with such a Lost, Missing or even DEPRESSED Pussy?!

Not many.

So they cum to me to help em find and retrieve the Spirit.

Sometimes men cum to me to help them as well.

4

The Spirit of DICKS goes missing too for a lotta the same fucked up reasons it happens with wommin.

And not to mention, the Government is bizzy replacing the Soul of Niggaz Dicks as much as possible, too.

There is a vast world conspiracy been going on since the 1920s to keep Black Men frum being born with da Essence of they Family Jewels intact.

At any rate, I send those cases to mah good friend and sumtime Lover, MADAME X (who U will meet later).

Im expensive.

I gits at least HALF mah money upfront.

And I git to keep as many PICTURES of da Pussy as I want to for further research.

I study Pussy intensively cuz its the onliest way U kan git to Know Pussy.

You may be thinking Im just a FREAK.

True.

What kan I say?

I fly mah Freak Flag high.

Butt Im also dam good at what I do.

2

It was anutha scorching, hot summer day on the SOUTH SIDE of ST. LOUIS and I had just got outta sum Pussy in mah office.

LENA Pussy.

Thats whose it was.

I Had been fucking LENA wit a type-a-Vengeance I reserve for mah Enemies.

And she had loved it.

Its mah favorite thing to do between cases of finding LOST PUSSY.

That is to say, I FUCK pussy when I dont have a case to FIND a pussy.

While Lena was gitting dressed to leave, I noticed a woman outside mah office reading the sign on the door.

REVEREND DADDY HOODOO: PUSSY DETECTIVE

She stood there a good five minutes just reading.

I presumed she was making up her mind.

Then: she knocked.

Cum In.

I drew the word out so that it sounded like: *Cummmmm In.*

She Entered.

She was light, bright and damn near White wit a Creole vibe about her.

And I had to keep mah composure as she was thick as old skool garlic baloney.

Her ass nearly hung to da back of her knees inside a Prince Purple-colored thin butt form-fitting Sun Dress.

Thru the back of her dress, I saw sweat running down the crack of her butt as she entered, turned around to look the place over.

I wanted to be That SWEAT.

She spoke.

Are U Reverend Daddy Hoodoo ?

Last I checked.

Well, I hope so because you cum highly recommended.

Thats good to know. By who?

Madame X. She said you help women with their Pussies, right?

True. I do. If the Price is right. And for all the pictures of said Pussy as possible.

She said you would say that.

Um-Hm. U good with that?

Yes, I am. I'm desperate to git mines back.

Oh, so Im like a last resort?

No, its not like that. I just didnt know about you before this.

I kan digg it. Well, peeple find me when they need to find me, I guess. But now that you have found me, have a seat and tell me what happened.

3

Lenas undulating ass, smelled of Afrikan Shea Butter and Black Soap, as she sashayed towards the door.

See you later, Daddy.

She stopped — and kissed me on the cheek.

Alrite, gul.

Miss You til I kiss you, Daddy.

Likewise, baby.

And She was gone.

Meanwhile, Abysinnia sat down at an angle and faced me with her knees slightly parted.

It was then that I smelled it.

The Faint Aroma of PANTYLESS Pussy.

I didnt know if she whudden wearing any to make me more apt to take on her case or if she was simply in mourning.

Because I done known women who go pantyless when they feeling some kinda way over the missing of they Pussy.

Then too, there are some women who wear no panties because they just sum slick WITCHES out on the prowl for a lustful night.

And going Pantyless lets the juices of the Honey Pot seep out and catch wind in some unsuspecting SIMP Nostrils.

Next thang U know da Po Nigga SUCCUMBS.

I have also known Witchy Women who even putt Pussy juices behind their ears like perfume.

And when a Nigga hugs or kisses them up close He gits a Sniff and a Whiff of that Thang.

And once again cums under her Spell.

See, Pheromones kan have a powerful aphrodisiac effect on a Nigga olfactory system causing it to go buck wild.

At any rate, I knew the unmistakeable smell of raw, wet pussy.

No panties, huh?

She was surprised.

How could you tell?

Its a gift. Plus, I got a sensitive nose, baby.

Well, I never liked wearing panties. I like my cookie to be free.

God is Good.

She laffed.

All The Time.

She finished my thought.

And Thank You. You're welcum.

Indeed. But go head didnt mean to interrupt ya.

Well, I woke up this Morning — and reached down to masturbate. Sumtimes I like to play with myself in the mornings before I go to work. Butt I could tell something wasnt right. And I've never experienced that before in my entire life of having a pussy.

Hmmmm. And how long have you had one?

You mean my age, right?

Rite.

25 years.

Scorpio?

Yes, how did you — ?

Like I said, its a Gift, baby. Matter of fact, a lotta what I do is beyond human komprehension. And everything I do I caint explain nor do I have time to clarify all that I do. You must trust the process. More importantly, you must trust ME.

That wont be a problem. I understand. And I'm prepared to Trust you as much as possible. I'm just ready to re-locate myself. I've never had this happen and Im scared as fuck, Reverend Daddy Hoodoo.

Solid. I think I kan help you find it. Butt meanwhile, there aint no guarantee tho.

4

A sad look came over Abysinnia face.

So I explained further.

Pussy cums and pussy goes. And sometimes it dont wanna cum back.

Well, cant you MAKE it cum back, Reverend Daddy Hoodoo?

I dont do that. And just call me DADDY.
Butt nobody kan make The Pussy cum back if it dont want to. And My policy is never to force. If it dont happen naturally, then, it just aint happening. You gotta understand that this might happen with you is all Im saying.

In other words, dont git my hopes up?

If its to be — it WILL be. Trust the process.

She nodded in the affirmative.

Now what?

Well, now Imma hit this weed. It helps me think.

You sharing, Daddy?

She smiled with a perfect row of chiclet-white teeth.

Sho nuff. U know It aint no fun if homie dont git none, rite?

Ko-rrect!

She smiled again with those Pearly Whites that belonged in a toothpaste commercial recommended by 4 out of 5 doctors or sum shit like dat.

I pulled a Newport Blunt out of a new pack I had just bought last nite.

Ever since the government had legalized Weed in every corner of Amerikkka these Newports had become my drug habit of choice.

Twenty-Two joints in a pack.

Two different strengths.

Regular Weed and Loud strength.

I liked the Regular over the Loud strength.

The Loud Weed made me wanna do something strange for a little bit-a-change.

And I didnt like that feeling.

KnowwhatImean?

I blew a ring of smoke in her direction hoping she would get a contact high, loosen up some more and show me even more of dat Puss Eye (my slang name for the goodness between a woman's legs) I was smelling.

She had that strong, funky, bushy-smelling pussy, too.

And I knew like I knew nothing else that I wanted to eat her or Finger her at a minimum.

However, I kept all that to the side as I turned her case over in mah mind.

I exhaled and passed the Joint to Her.

I said: The government and these tobacco companies are now making more money off of Marijuana Joints than Cigarettes.

She was on the inhale and simply nodded her head at my words. As she blew out the smoke I inhaled it from her.

Butt seconds later:

I noticed.

We took turns passing the Joint back and forth.

I continued rapping to her between hits.

So, listen, if we do this you gotta be ready to accept what I tell ya.

I was blowing smoke directly in her face.

And she returned the favor.

Whether you believe it or not is on you. But your response will determine whether or not we go further or stop altogether.

Nah, I wanna do this, Daddy.

She spoke between Puffs.

Thats good.

But how did you as a man git into this line of work?

Like I said, its a GIFT.

Umph.

She hit the Joint again.

So its your gift to know pussy?

She struggled to hold in the smoke.

Basically. Its what I do. In fact, BORN to do. I Know pussy. I Talk to pussy. And I FIND pussy.

Wow. Im impressed as fuck.

Well, I do what I kan. Studying pussy is an ancient art. And its very POLITICAL. Butt then — You probably know that.

She nodded.

SEX is Power. U ever heard that phrase?

Yes. I've also heard of Pussy Power, too.

Rite. Well, there you go. Thats why a lotta people actually FEAR pussy. They dont understand its deeper artistic meaning or its political power.

And that makes them scared of it?

AbSOULutely. People fear what they dont understand — and that definitely includes Pussy.

Thats deep. Why do you think its like that tho?

Cuz The PTBs dont wanna ever again wanna see Pussy control Men folk like it once did.

The PTBs?

The Powers That Be. The fools who run the world. Mostly MEN. Butt with help from of a lotta Women, too.

They keep the status quo going?

Exactly.

And my Pussy kan actually feel all that? What? Like in a metaphysical sense?

I could see she was definitely INQUISITIVE and CONCERNED as a muthafucka.

She was looking hard at me through the weed smoke filling up my office.

Um-Hm. And like in a REAL sense too. Yo Pussy Essence is as real as YOU are. It Is its OWN BEING. Its just located DOWN there.

I pointed underhand at her crotch, palm facing upwards.

It was an Occult salute — and a bit of Feng Shui, the ancient art of directing energy wherever you wanted it to go.

So this is NOT a game, huh?

Nah, baby. What I do is as real as it gets. Thats why you gotta go hard into this and dont Flake out on me. Becuz you gone have to git Naked in mo ways than just Physical, ya digg? And we gone open A Portal for some answers.

Im down with whatever you need me to do, Daddy.

Dig dat. Does yo pussy have a Name?

Yes. Harmony.

The world dam sho needs mo of dat.

I need that in my life for sure. In my relationships.

Sho nuff. Every woman deserves that.

You are only the 2nd man I've told her Name to.

Why is that?

Because my Granny told me never to reveal the name of your Pussy to a Man. Less you want him to control you.

I see Granny was smart. Cuz dat shit kan cum back and Haunt You. Naming thangs is sum very Powerful shit. And a Womayne sho nuff gotta be Kareful who knows da Name of Dat THANG.

I know you not lying, Daddy. I cant say I always listened to my Granny. And maybe thats the problem now. So I have to give her that. But she aint never taught me nothing on the level of what you are saying about my Pocketbook now.

I waited a beat. Then:

You feel uncomfortable gitting this type of info from a Man?

Truth be told, on my way here I was feeling some kinda way at first. But the way you rapping to me I kan see how it makes sense. And anyway, Im for anybody that kan help me. Period. Male or Female.

Rite on. I had to ask becuz many wommin dont like it.

Thats THEIR loss.

I nodded.

Aight, so you woke up this morning and Yo Pussy was gone?

Um-Hm. I had had sex the night before.

Why did I get jealous as a Muthafucka all of a sudden?

I knew better than that shit!!

Umph. Is that rite?

Yeah. You think that had something to do with it? Cuz the Brotha I was with is the only other man that knows my Girls name.

Hmmmm. Maybe. It depends. Go on. Did you cum?

She shifted in her seat some more and I could have sworn I heard her plump ass plop 2gether under her dress.

My mind was probably just playing tricks on me tho since the scent of this woman was all up in mah Nostrils.

I always cum. Even if I have to do it myself. Which is usually what happens. Because Its not easy for a man to make me have an orgasm. Butt yes. I did cum with him.

Did HE Cum inside U?

Yes. He did.

Umph.

Is that a problem?

Possible. Depends on the rest of ya story.

She continued the Deets.

*Well, we fucked. We got in a big argument. And then I kicked
him out.*

Why?

U mean why did I kick him out?

Yeah.

Dont hold this against me, Daddy, butt I like being with
more than one man.

I dont judge, baby. I do Pre-Judge though. Saves me the time
of dealing with lousy muthafuckaz. So he wanted it to be
just you and him. But you wasnt feeling that.

*No, he wanted it be just Me, Him and his OTHER Wives, too. Which
I dont mind as long as I kan see other Men as well. I was honest
about that and he didnt like it. Butt I've always been into Polyamory.*

Everythang aint for everybody. I guess he aint realize that.

*No he did not. But I have. And Im done with that. I tried monogamy.
And it doesn't work for me.*

I realized my Dick had never been as hard as it was rite now.

Just the way her perfect teeth came 2gether as she spoke
honestly to me made sumthing run thru me.

She stood up and her body was Pornographically Beautiful
in its Proportions.

I dont think she meant to tease me — but it is what it is.
The woman was ridiculously deelishis.

Something wrong?

I thought maybe she could tell how Ignant mah Dick was
acting for her inside mah pants.

No, I just need to run to the bathroom right quick.

Out the door and to the right, down the hall on the left.

Be right back.

Her titties nearly bounced out the top of her dress as she
strode out of my office to the bathroom.

She left the office smelling of lavender oil and pheromones.

Before I realized it she was back.

So do you think you kan help me git Harmony back?

Well, like I said, we gone give it a dam good try. Cuz
nothing beats a failure but a try, rite?

True.

I need to holla at Madame X about you, first.

*Be my guest. Because I aint got nothing to hide. That's for damn sure.
Im so ready to git my Kitty-Kat back to its rightful place it aint even
funny.*

I believe you. But hold dat thought. And lets rap later.

We hugged.

My Dick pressed into her soft, womanly flesh as we hugged.

I know she could feel it. But she didnt even flinch.

I broke the hug off abruptly cuz it felt like I was about to
bust a nut on myself like a Lame Nigga.

Check with you later, Daddy.

She flashed the 4 out of 5 doctors-approved smile again.

Her breath smelled like fresh, 2-percent milk.

I watched her ass cheeks appear to be fighting to git out of
her tight dress as she bopped away in what seemed like slow
motion — and into my life.

I had never been mo ready to SOLVE a case.

And FUCK.

5

Madame X had been born and blessed with having one of the HOTTEST Pussies known to Man.

She always said she was Born to be a Hoe and A Madam.

And so it came to Pass as it was written in da Stars.

Her Hoe Activities flourished.

One day she told me:

I came here to fuck.

No doubt she was Destined.

20 years of Hoeing later and she was now the proud Madame & Owner of a series of Brothels and Exotic Massage Parlors through-out the State of Missouri (aka Misery).

This kept her in the position of being able to manage (and watch out for) hundreds of wayward girls who often wound up on the streets for one reason or another (usually Sex

Trafficking at the hands of Psychotic Pimps....I will tell U bout one of those krazy Pimps soon)

But Lucky for these girls Madame was holding it down.

Becuz no one was better at taking a young girl off the streets and helping em git their lives 2gether to be Productive Members (and Hoes) of Society — all while making hundreds of dollars in unreported income.

Doing it THEY Way instead of being abused by the Flesh Peddling Pimps who useta have them.

Me and Madame had had a sweet, beautiful affair a long time ago.

But never stopped loving and caring about each other.

She has been the only woman I know that made me believe in love again.

Her house was in the ritzy central west end section of St. Louis.

Actually, make that a MANSION — not a house.

I could always find her at home — or traveling to visit one of her Brothels or reiki centers.

No matter where she was, she was surrounded by women and gossip.

She knew more about what was going on in St. Louis than anybody — often including the Police.

If Madame X didnt know about it then — it wasnt worth knowing.

So I was curious as to why she thought Abysinnia was worth my time.

<hr>

My cellphone rang.

I snatched it into my hand.

Whats happening Big Mama Almighty?

It was Madame X.

Big Mama Almighty was mah nickname for her because she one of them type of Big Legged woman like all them old skool Big Mamas we grew up with.

Thick and Short. Stout. And the Biggest, prettiest leggs U ever wanna see.

The kind I loved to spread back over a woman head.

She said: I got your thought-form!

I see.

When we were together some years ago, we useta fuck like rabbits — and we were always sending one another thought forms about one thing or another:

Pick up sum OJ frum da store; Meet you at da Casino for dinner and gambling; or Dont cum home — the Police are here lookin for you.

We had been that way ever since we used to git down in the sheets.

Our relationship had been almost telepathic.

27

In fact, it was still that way.

Its like we were born as Siamese Twins or Soulmates.

Then, Separated.

And came back 2gether as Lovers.

And now as Friends. For Ever.

I couldnt do this work without her.

I depended on her to case the mental of any woman that needed mah services.

I knew my weakness — and truth be told — sometimes I let my Dick git in the way of taking a womans case.

Madame had no such problem.

I knew I could git the straight shit from her.

About anything.

Especially, women.

Im on my way to see you about Abysinnia.

I'll be here, Lover.

We still called each other dat word.

Old habits die hard, I guess.

Noted. I be there in bout 60 minutes of Nigga Peeples Time.

Aight, Daddy. See U then.

6

_____

I put on mah Git-A-Nigga-Out-of-Jail-Suit.

Steel, gray, somewhat shiny.

Expensive.

Every time I hit them streets I was dressed to impress fo success, baby, Ya digg?

I Had to be Suited and Booted.

Clothes right.

Shoes tight.

A knot (of Money) in my pocket.

I dont fuck wit credit cards.

Cuz they never really give you credit.

Only a Debit when that bill came due 30 days.

And one thang I dont need is another Bill.

I rarely kept ONES on me.

Mah Daddy tole me: *Dollar Bills were for chumps.*

I liked counting my money in Fives.

KnowwhatImean?

Whenever I did have Ones on me it was mostly to pass out to homeless Niggaz.

Plus, they watched my Back — and the Streets for me.

Fair exchange aint no robbery is sumpen else mah Daddy always told me.

I lived by that.

I checked my teeth in the mirror.

I still had a decent amount of whiteness on mah 50 year old Fangs.

I had been using that Colgate Tooth Whitener.

That shit worked.

Plus, I had stopped drinking coffee — unless I was fucking.

Cuz then it acted like Cialis or Viagra.

At least wit me it did.

My head was bald.

Always.

I had fought the bald look all the way.

And Lost.

Cuz once I started getting a hole in my Natural (I used to have a beautiful afro)— I decided to just go with the flow.

The ladies loved it.

And that's all that mattered.

Plus a blessing came with the tragic loss of my Afro.

I learned to do some sexual things with a bald head in the bedroom that had begun to make me legendary.

My Goatee was properly coiffed.

Check.

My Daddy had left me a purple, 56s, convertible Caddy with white wall tires.

I had the muthafucka modified and brought up to date.

Sirius radio and GPS and that kinda shit.

Ya follow me?

In short, I was ready for the world, baby.

Time to see my gul Madame X.

The baddest Unbothered Bitch that I knew.

And who I was still in love with after all these years in my own way.

Even tho we wasnt technically a couple.

We were still a couple (if you catch my meaning).

In the car I turned my Sirius Radio on and danced between Stations 49 and 50 for that old school shit.

I always went between those two stations.

Every now and then I switched to station 42 for some Reggae.

But that was mainly to see if old school reggae was playing.

I didnt like that new reggae shit that had started cumming out after Bob Marley and Peter Tosh died.

White folks fuck up everything.

Im not being racist when I say this.

Butt its just true.

White folks fuck up soul music when they git a hold of it.

At any rate, I liked all my music old school style is all I meant.

The best fucking songs are all old school.

And I couldnt fuck to this new shit they played on the radio nowdays.

Its just something bout how older music was made that made it easier for a Nigga like me to catch his STROKE.

And the women that I had been with loved it when they caught the riddim of my stroke as I fucked da shit out of em.

When I was on my game I would stay on the edge of Busting a nut all nite long — except I didnt.

Of course, it didnt always work out like that becuz the PUSSY is all-powerful, yaheahme?

And erry now n then a Nigga would bust-a-nut within 5 minutes of entering that hot muthafucka!

Nevertheless, gimme that old time music, baby.

I flipped the station to 49 and there Al Green was singing one of mah favorite joints: *Something.*

My mind wandered to Abysinnia.

She had one of those asses that was BIG for no reason (as I called em).

The kinda ass that made you wanna stick yo head in her butt cheeks and sniff her crack — and eat da HOLE out da muthafucka.

Just because.

What kan I say?

I tole U Imma Freak.

AND — I mite be what U kall NASSY-as-a-Muthafucka, too.

So in my mind Im thinking why somebody as fine as her would be having these issues.

Butt see, you never know bout sumbody.

They kan be looking FINE on da outside and be tore up from da floor up on da inside with sum bullshit.

Als crooning broke into mah thoughts with da bridge of da song....I nodded a minute in time wit da hook...

Back to Abysinnia.

She was an Amazon too.

Dam near 6 feet tall.

My cellphone rang again.

Yeah, baby?

Daddy?

It was Madame.

You on da way?

Yeah.

I need to run out around the corner for a minute but I will be back before you git here.

Solid, Lover. Im there in about another 10 mins.

Okay.

I decided to finish my daydreaming about Abysinnia later — and enjoy the rest of my ride over lost in the songs on the radio.

Patti LaBelle was singing that dam *Lady Marmalade* that I never learned the words to.

All I knew was Itchy-Itchy coo and thats it.

I knew one thing: Cant-A-Bitch OUT-SANG Patti.

Maybe ARETHA.

Butt Patti range was off da charts.

Made mah Dick Hard.

Actually, a lotta things made my Johnson hard.

But only as it related to Women n shit.

What can I say?

I'm built funny.

However, it also contributed to me being damn good at what I do.

You see, My Dick has actually helped me solve a lot of the cases I done been on.

So I learned to value its Counsel.

And over the years it has usually been right about so much shit it aint even funny.

If mo men listened to their Dick they would have less problems.

Guaranteed.

Sure, sum Dicks have gone rogue.

But many more are astute in their assessment of a number of predicaments a man might find himself in.

Wise would be the man to take heed to the Profundity of The Penis.

This phenomena is, in fact, very similar to the ones women have with their Vee-Jay-Jay as well.

Butt as I told you I let Madame X handle all Dick cases.

One of these days I will share with you some stories of those male potency issues.

Courtesy of Madame X.

7

I arrived at MADAME X.

I took the steps up to her joint.

I heard her distinctive voice as I strode down the hallway on the way to her door.

Madame X got one of dem stocky, Five Feet-Four Inch builds and short dreadlocks.

As I came to her doorway She was rapping to a Sistar (as she calls ALL women).

I paused, leaning in the doorway to let her finish.

Listen to me, My Sistar. What matters most is how you feel about it not how everyone else feels about it.

I know you absolutely right Madame X. Im going to handle it just like you said.

The sweet, brown-skinned honey was smiling approval.

Madame X nodded and smiled in return.

May I have one of your famous hugs before I leave, Mama?

Lotta the Younger guls called Her Mama.

Girl, yes. Come here.

Madame X and the woman bear hugged one another.

They both make a sound like they were having a simultaneous ORGASM.

Uhhhhhhhhhhhh!!!!

Woman: Thank you.

Madame X: You're welcome, Sistar. See you next time.

The fine, sweet, brown-skin Honey left and nodded to Me as she walked by.

Madame walked over to me.

Can I have one of those too?

What? A Hug or My Sistar?

She knew me too well.

I played it off.

Nah, just a Hug, baby.

Big Smile.

You know you can always git one of those, Daddy.

Madame came into my arms.

Just da way I like it.

Um-Hm. I know how you LIKE it. Up in them Stomach Muscles.

Dadd-d-d-d-d-y! You so Mannish.

I was born Mannish, baby. U know that.

I know. I like when You Mannish too. And you know I miss you being all up in my Stomach Muskles!

We said Muscles wit a K cuz we loved being Ebonically Incorrect.

Um-Hm. I bet you do. Butt in the Mean Time and Between Time whats up wit Abysinnia?

8

Did I tell you me and Madame X still fucked every now and then?

Yeah We Do.

We gits it in.

Sumtimes like Rabbits.

Butt more often like 2 slowly, entertwined, languorous Snakes.

Even tho we aint officially a couple no mo.

Like I said earlier, We useta fuck a LOT.

But now we just fuck OFTEN.

Which is to say still a lot but not a lot, lot if you git my meaning.

Why?

Becuz good pussy is hard to come by—especially when you

find one that FITS.

And Madame X's still fit me like a glove.

Of course, I already told you how hot her pocket was, too, right?

I remember when ever (or where ever) we useta git down, Madame loved how I would push my Big Dick as far up in her as I could get it—and still today she loves that shit.

PUT IT IN MY STOMACH MUSKLES, DADDY!!!!

She used to holla as I ran my pipe deep into her--and pulled it out slowly so she could see all her JUICES on it.

She loved it DEEP up in her Belly.

And all these years later I still aint found a woman who could take This Vitamin D like I likes to give it to Madame.

Thats why I aint stopped jumping between the sheets with her yet.

And probably never will.

So about Abysinnia?

She good, Daddy.

Still always calling me DADDY.

She never gave a damn what other women thought about her calling me Daddy.

Madame called me Daddy ANYWHERE.

In Public.

In the World.

In front of dignataries or public officials.

It didnt matter who or where.

Her attitude has always been FUCK em.

Thats one of da main reasons I was krazy bout her.

She aint have no Filter.

You sure she aint no krazy bitch? You know many of dem caint handle the process of opening up a portal.

No. She good, Daddy. I promise you. I talked to her for a good minute before I sent her your way.

I just nodded.

Because I knew I could count on Madame.

Her word was Bond—which is why I would give mah Life for Madame X.

You would just be back to this realm, she often said since she believed in reincarnation.

And I believed that shit, too.

I just always been one of those people who felt one lifetime wasnt enough to finish all the shit I had to do.

So I had to cum back and finish administering the proper amount of ass whuppings to said enemies—or loving to said Women Folk.

Aight. If you say so then dat shit IS so, baby.

Heah the thing tho:

Madames Kryptonite was her extreme Kindness and Faith in Humans. Those were problems I didnt have.

True, I believed in helping women find their Sacred Places, ya digg?

But at the same time I turned down lots of Pussies over the years, too.

Madame X, on the other hand—hell, she believed in Everybody.

Meanwhile, I didnt believe in Anybody but myself for the most part.

And basically, that was the toughest part about being in a relationship with her.

Despite her brilliant intuition, she trusted the wrong people too much.

The result of that was I wound up cleaning up the damage more than I had a mind to.

Still, in the great cosmic scheme of things—it was minor.

I didnt mean to make it sound like more than it is.

Just an observation and a desire for her to cure that issue one day.

I know she will.

In other words, all in all, I would still take Madame any day over the rest of the entire world on my side, ya understand me?

So Abbysinnia knows the play?

Yes, Daddy.

You dont have any doubts about her?

No, Daddy. None that I would question.

How long have you known her?

*About 6 months. I met her thru a Sensuous Asian Massage class I
was giving at the University.*

I knew the University.

Washington University aka WASH U.

It was one of them Jewish schools for rich white kids,
mostly.

They would let-a-Nigga in here and there to break the color
barrier though—and to Fuck da White Girls with them fat
Trust Funds.

The Sistas was gitting it in too with all them White Boys
looking for a Mammy.

Madame was an instructor of Asian Massage Classes there.

White folks love asian shit.

Hell, Asian ANYTHING.

And Asian Massage was no exception.

You cant keep white peeple away from that shit.

So that just meant Madame stayed paid in the shade teaching at that joint.

A lotta Creoles and Niggaz passing for WHITE went there too for one reason or another.

They whudden all necessarily attending the College.

They was just going there cuz Wash U got all types of community education they offer to ANYBODY.

So dats what Abysinnia was doing there.

Taking Madames community Workshop.

Not long after that she went Missing DOWN There.

Thats when she turned to Madame.

And Madame turned to me.

Truth be told, I aint lost a Pussy yet.

Aight. Imma take her case on it.

Madame had cleared up other questions I had about Abysinnia.

With me it was all bout TRUST.

If a woman couldnt be trusted to be stable during this process I didnt want to be bothered.

I done seen too many Women have nervous breakdowns behind the type of Full out RITUAL Process I was about to put Abysinnia through.

I didnt need or WANT that shit on my conscious.

9

I made it back to mah office.

I had agreed to see Abysinnia on the Strength of Madame X say-so.

This bizness had taught me dat TRUSTED word of Mouf is da best way to do thangs.

Ion even trust mah Own MAMA for sertain thangs.

So I know I aint gone trust da AVERAGE Muthafucka about too much.

I trusted Madame X tho.

Lets be CLEAR bout Sumpen: If you cant trust the Woman or Man you having SEX wit — you FUCKIN Up.

Butt that shit is like RARE AIR that most people ain't used to Breathing, baby.

It dont exist for the most part.

This is why one of the MAIN problems wit Women and they Missing PUSSIES is they place DA PUSS EYE in the TRUST- -and CARE of a Nigga who never should have had the Goodness in the First Place.

Truth Be Tole: Women are a BAD Judge of Character.

Most Women reading those werds just disagreed wit me.

Butt my Bizness of Finding Lost and Missing Pussies says OTHERWIZE.

Women know each other — butt MANY of them cant see a NO GOOD Nigga cumming until he done GOT da Punany.

Next thang you know, they have a Nuclear FALL OUT.

Shit hits da Fan.

The Relationship or whatever da fuck you wanna call what they THOUGHT they had is OVER.

And next thang you know They calling Me wit a Pussy Issue.

Innerstand Me.

Course, I know WHAT a woman does wit HER Pussy is ultimately HER bizness (Im very clear on that. And been clear on that for YEARS).

BUTT —

I know PEEPLES, POWER and PUSSY in an INTIMATE way.

Dont ask me HOW I know.

I just know.

And my work over da years has beared dat shit out.

So I knew exactly what Abysinnia was going through — and a lotta of What was behind da shit.

10

————

I putt the call into Abysinnia on mah landline (yeah, I still got one cuz the muthafucka is dependable).

HELLO, Daddy.

She answered on the 2nd ring.

Its time to go DEEPER, baby.

Im ready. Just tell me when and Where.

Back here at My Office. In My Sanctuary. A few days from now.

Got it. Should I wear anything particular?

I WANTED to tell her dont WEAR SHIT BABY.
JUST ARRIVE IN THIS MUTHAFUCKA BUCKED NEKKID.

Butt what I said was: Just Dress Comfortable. And dont eat. Just drink water all that day.

Okay, Daddy. just FAST all that day. Got it.

She said it like we were Fucking.

And it sounded so god-dam sexy.

See you then.

I was about to hang up.

She stopped Me.

DADDY!

Yeah, baby?

So what did Madame X say? If you dont mind me asking.

She said ENUFF. Butt I will tell you more about that when we git 2Getha.

Alright. I will see you then.

Lata.

In fact, in hindsight, I realized Madame X had tole me way more than I thought.

She had mentioned The Nigga she had seen Abysinnia with on a few occasions at Washington University.

You know his Name, I asked?

Nah, Daddy. You know Me. I dont Pry in anutha Bitch life if she dont invite me to. So I never asked her bout him.

Hmmm. What he look like?

He was kinda Shifty-lookin if you ask me. Jet Black type-a-Nigga. A little Taller than you.

I had to admit that sounded like a BUNCH O' Niggaz, really.

He had was Shiny too. Like the Nigga had too much Vaseline on him or sumpen. She laffed.

And just like dat Madame X had narrowed it down.

I thought I knew who she was talkin bout now.

Thats sumpen else I loved about Madame.

She didnt miss shit.

She had Rabbit Eyes.

Could see 360 degrees in all directions.

She read my thought.

You know I dont MISS SHIT, Daddy.

I just smiled at the Intrusion into my Brain.

Abysinnia had never tole me da Nigga name.

And I didnt ask.

I like peeple to Volunteer shit for me to know otherwize I figger I dont need to know.

I would ask her the next time we got 2gether.

Because IF it WAS who I THOUGHT it was we were gonna have to do more than just open a Portal in my Sanctuary.

Meanwhile, I got up and walked over to the Bookcase in my office.

After talkin to Abysinnia I knew JUST da Book I wanted to consult for first
Reference.

It was called PUSSY THROUGH THE AGES by DOCTOR SUN STAR DIVINE.

And had been written in 1848.

According to Niggatel, Doctor Sun Star was one of da first to brang SEX MAJICK to Amerikkka way back in the 1800s in New Orleans (more on dat lata).

Ironically, it was in New Orleans where I had paid a Nigga $5,000 in Legal Tender for da joint when I was on a case sum years ago in the French Quarter.

In fact, I had copped 2 books that trip.

Anutha one called The HOLY BOOK OF NIGGAMASTE.

It was an ancient Bible that Niggaz of a sertain Master Teacher background used to order life.

My Bookcase was one of those old skool joints where you hit da Button and it mooved outta da way to reveal an OPENING behind it.

I had it designed dat way so I could bail outta my office without being noticed if I needed to. Or even HIDE frum Muthafuckaz I aint wanna see.

There were TWO more floors underneath the bookcase.

There was a Deep underground area there.

I called it My SANCTUARY.

And its where I did mah Rituals.

And it was LAID OUT.

There were Rows of Ancient Books on SEX and SEX MAJICK and other Forms of Wizdom and Old Art Work.

I had AMULETS & HAND-WRITTEN SACRED MANTRAS n shit frum all around da world frum da places I had traveled doing my work.

I Collected em.

Many were Given to Me in Thanks and Favors.

Sum I paid for.

Others I stole.

What kan I say?

Imma Nigga.

I steal.

Butt I only STEAL BACK whats rightfully Mines.

And belongs to Niggaz.

Because when You THINK about it — all KNOWLEDGE cums back to Niggaz.

I had one of the Deepest BLACK EROTICA FOLKLORE Collections in the World.

Most of the world thinks the ASIANS created this SEX shit.

Not So.

Therefore, not many muthafuckaz know dat it was Niggaz dat actually Invented all this Sacred Sexual Art shit like Tantra, Kama Sutra and Ananga Ranga — and just plain old GOOD Fucking.

Then we wrote BOOKS and Drew PICTURES about da Shit — and HID it.

And forgot.

Just kept it in our DNA, ya feel me?

See, Our Ancestors knew the Average Muthafucka wasnt ready for dat type of Fucking.

They also knew E-vil Muthafuckaz would try to take da SECRETS and ABUSE em as a form of SEXUAL KONTROL over both Women AND Men.

And thats JUST what happened.

We were told tole to Guard The Knowledge wit Our Lives.

We Did.

We Lost.

The shit got out.

And INTO da WRONG Hands of The DIABOLIKAL ONES.

Thats why I considered it my Sacred and Sworn Duty to GIT back as much of dat shit as possible.

By Any Means Necessary.

The way I seent it: They STOLE IT. BUT WE MUST
RETURN IT, baby.

Unto its RITEFUL place in Niggaz Lives.

11

I dont eat when Im gitting ready to Rescue Pussy.

What dat does dat MEAN?

That means Im gitting ready to open a PORTAL (thats what I call going in search of da Pussy thru an Elaborate Ritual I put a Woman thru to make contact wit da Spirit of The Puss Eye proper, ya digg)?

Its all done in my Underground Sanctuary where its quiet as a muthafucka.

In other words, its SOUNDPROOF.

Its so quiet, You kan hear a Roach PISS in a Crack (yeah I got Roaches butt they aint outta kontrol).

Thats cuz Me and Roaches gots an Understanding: they dont cum out when I got a Client over for a Ritual).

In so many words, they Dont Fuck Wit Me—and I dont Fuck wit dem.

You Kan laff if U wants to BUTT Roaches are among the

most Intelligent Critters on da Planet fo real. (Its a good reason Roaches and Niggaz would be da only ones left on da Earth if a nuclear bomb ever dropped and wiped this Muthafucka OUT).

They just dont git the Respeck they deserve.

But over the years I've learned to Cummunicate wit em— and other Insects too.

I gits a Woman down in my Sanctuary and we go in DEEP.

Butt before all that happens I been done stopped eating for at least 24 to 36 hours prior to that.

This raises the Viberation of my Blood to an extremely, High SENSITIVE level.

Then, I hit da Weed for dat Next Level of Entry into da Mind. See, you gotta combine da two in da proper proportions.

I gits me dat Regular WEED tho.

Not this new shit thats outcheah — full of khemikals — and fucking up Niggaz Minds.

———

Thats da reason I also purchase mah Weed frum My Gul SONJA.

She is an Underground supplier who grows da shit herself in her own Farm Greenhouse — just like I likes it. (She even got Cops for Customers).

Cuz Imma Tell Ya — as a Rule, Ion trust these Progressive Strains of Weed they got outcheah now.

Dat shit got Niggaz SEEING Thangs dat aint even there!

I had one Nigga even tell me He felt He was turning GAY behind smoking this new Un-godly shit that dont nobody know what the hell they spraying on it!

And if its ONE Thang we dont need: its Mo BITCH NIGGAZ running round outcheah in deez streets.

Butt I digress.

Abysinnia was NEW to this while I was TRUE to this.

And Truth be Tole, I was worried she mite Freak out during da Ritual.

I dam sho was gone find out tho.

I needed to make sum quick runs before she came over in a few days.

12

————

I hit up SONJA bout dat Dose.

Sup baby? You got my normal Nigga Shit?

I KEEPS Yo Shit, Daddy, if I don't Keep NO BODY ELSES. When You cumming by?

In 15 mins or less.

It be here waiting on You. Just like this Pussy You keep running frum.

Ahaaaa. I laffed Hard.

Sonja was always tryna git me to HIT dat.

Butt I knew as soon as I knocked her off She would go Nuts. Cuz She was just dat Type. So I left dat door CLOSED.

Nah, You know Ion run frum PUSSY, gul. Pussy Runs Frum Me.

Yeah, butt Not THIS One.

True Story. Lemme PRAY first.

Now SHE laffed. HARD.

You A Mess, Rev!!

BASIKALLY. Aight. Imma see U in a few, baby.

Okay, Daddy.

I still had about 48 more hours or so before Me Abysinnia linked back up.

I putt on a RED SUIT.

I dont normally wear LOUD-Colored Clothes. Period.

Butt I was setting up mah RITUAL Vibe--Which when U doing U want ya Aura noticed by the Public cuz mite be a stranger need to katch that same Feeling for a HEALING, knowhutImean?

Really, da suit was Mo CRANBERRY Red.

A Somewhat Muted color butt still louder than I usually wore, ya understand?

I Crowned mah shit wit a Black Straw Hat.

The Shoes were Cranberry Leather.

Silk Cranberry Socks.

My T-Shirt and Drawls were silk, too.

Silk or Satin was all I wanted against my Skin.

Altho I did wear Cotton T-shirts round my office or home sometimes.

I got this dressing shit frum mah Daddy.

He never left da House unless he was Ready for Action.

He useta say: When you leave da house, boy, always be dressed to impress for success. Especially, when you bout to go git sum MONEY or—sum PUSSY. It pays to look like an IMPORTANT NIGGA.

I never forgot dat lesson.

I cant tell you how many times simply having on a Suit, lookin like an Important Nigga done got me both Money and Pussy — and maybe even Mo Important — got me ACCESS.

And in this World Today — A Nigga without ACCESS is A Nigga without SUC-CESS.

I needs and WANTS every ADVANTAGE I kan git doing this work I do.

Altho, Truth Be Tole — Not every Nigga in a Suit is bout shit.

I once saw a Nigga SAGGIN his pants in a Suit. (it was Summer & he had the suit coat slung over his shoulder).

Kan you bleeve THAT shit?!

Wit sum expensive ass STACY ADAMS on at that.

$400-Dollar shoes wit an Expensive suit — and this Nigga was showing his ass Crack!

Truly everybody aint able.

And MOST aint even WILLING.

This is one of the Mental Conditions dat hold Niggaz Down, keepin us chasing CRUMBS like BUMS.

Too many of My NIggaz done become LACKADAISICAL. APATHETIC.

I aint having it tho.

Especially when there is still work outcheah to be done — dealing with E-Vil Forces in High Places — whose main goal is to Snatch the Essence of Niggaz LOINS.

Cuz in Eyes of The Enemy a Nigga wit-a-DICK is considered being ARMED & DANGEROUS.

They want the BLACK Dick and Pussy rendered USELESS.

Believe Me when I tell you dat times like these have been MANIPULATED to Try Niggaz Souls.

Because the Bottom Line is da SOUL is what The Powers That Be WANT, ya understand?

If Niggaz aint gone be DETERMINED to Cum Out on TOP — we dam sho gone remain on da BOTTOM.

I hit da streets for dat Meet and Greet wit Sonja.

I had a Muthafuckin portal to open.

13

I sat thinking about fucking SONJA when I got in my ride.

Lawd knows I was tempted.

She was damn near CHARCOAL BLACK in complexion.

So Black you could barely see her at Nite.

And she was not just thick in the ass--she was Thick in da HIPPS.

So she had one of dem ASSES you could see cumming from The FRONT!

She was just BIG all over: Calves, Arms, neck...LIPS...the woman was just a Gift from the Gods.

She even had big TEETH.

The better to EAT you with Daddy, she would always say to me.

And I wanted her to eat me up too.

So I could consume her in return.

However what does it PROFIT a Nigga to gain a Whole Pussy but lose His SOUL?

I know what U saying: SUMPEN RONG WIT ME!

Prolly. Butt I couldnt take that chance with Sonja.

Because Sonja was Crazy with a Capital K.

She had stabbed several of her Lovers over the years—and did jail time.

Never killed none of dem Niggaz doe.

And I wasn't gonna be the FIRST.

Even though my skills for calming women folk down was unparalleled, I just wasn't in the mood to take that chance with Krazy Sonja.

No matter how tempting it was.

And no matter how often she told me she had been celibate now for the last 6 years.

Irregardless, I had to pass on that ass for the time being.

Even tho a couple of times I had grown weak for Her (especially, after I had got a Whiff of her Pheromones).

She had one of the strongest natural scents of any woman I had done come across.

So on a few occasions I ALMOST took Sonja up on her offer.

I remember the conversation that almost got me to git down and nasty with her.

We were in my car chain-smoking one Blunt after another.

And Sonja had her hand on my Dick.

I want this, she said, squeezing mah Jimmy, firmly.

Nah, baby, you know we cant git down like that.

Come on Daddy you know it's been a long minute for me. And I dont wanna just be with ANY man. I wanna be with YOU.

Why ME, baby?

Cuz you the perfect Nigga to knock the Bottom outta this Pussy. You truly got that Majick Stick.

I laffed.

Yeah, but once I give you some of this loving are you gone up and STAB-a-Nigga, baby?

Now, it was HER turn to laff loudly for a good minute.

After she caught her Breath she said:

Why would I do that to you, Daddy? You aint like them other lames I was dealing with. They were Bitch-Niggaz that crossed a sertain threshhold with me—and had to be dealt with.

She was squeezing mah Shit as she talked—and looking at me with so much lust my Dick developed a heart beat in time with her grip.

I NEED this Daddy. I really do. And you the ONLY Nigga I wanna do this with at this time in my life.

Her words were convincing.

Her rap was beautiful.

It was like listening to music.

And mah John Shaft was hard up against the inside of mah pants.

Then, I watched as she pulled her long dress up over her knees and gently slid a finger into her Pussy and brought it back out—and stuck it into my mouf.

I sucked her finger real smooth like.

So yeah THAT day I was TEMPTED.

But a Man like me cant do this work if he cant kontrol his Lower Nature.

If I cant Think for Mah Dick more than Mah Dick THINKS for Me, I already know what happens when One succumbs to a life of Unkontrolled LUST.

One, Ultimately, Leads a LIFE out of Kontrol as well his.

I done seen it happen to those kontrolled by the forces that take over their LOINS.

It is said that there are 72 Goetia Demons & Gods that reside in every Man NUTS.

And Influence how you respond to the Lure of Sex.

In other words, is Your INTENT worth the FUCK?

Is it a simple one-nite stand to bust-a-nut or are you

grinding out some MAJICK with A Woman who actually means SOMETHING to You.

Hear me on this.

It makes-a-difference.

These Demons or Gods are given priority based on how they are used.

The more power you give to baseless sex the more powerful the Demons become and kontrol your Nature.

Many become Nymphs with no ability to kontrol who or where they fuck.

I whudden sure what SONJA meant to me just yet.

Was she gone be just-a-fuck OR a Gateway to something powerful that we BOTH needed and desired?

———

I realized I had been sitting in the car for over half an hour already, lost in Mah thawts bout Sonja.

I started the car up.

The engine purred thanks to Mah Nigga BENNY.

He kept mah shit running smooth and without problems.

I never had to worry bout dat god-dam Check Engine Light coming on--which was a pure scam by the auto industry. (remind to tell you bout that at anutha time)

The Nigga could take a car apart and putt it back 2getha again in His SLEEP.

He never went to Skool for da shit either.

Didnt I Blow Yo Mind this time (by The Delfonics) were the words that wailed from the song as the Sirius Radio kicked in, automatically.

It was just what I wanted to ride to as I pulled out and massaged mah way into evening Traffick to go see Sonja's fine, troublesome ass about mah customized GANJA.

14

St Louis got that hot, sticky weather that keeps ya drawls
(or panties) glued or knotted up in ya ass like they got
sumpen against ya.

Summer is muggy cuz of the humidity carried by the Mighty
Mississippi River and peeple stay mad a lot cuz its so
damn hot.

But the evening traffick weather be the worst cuz of the
fumes, too.

Yeah, I coulda let mah windows up.

But truth be told, Ion like airconditioning.

Guess cuz I was raised mostly without it in the car.

Mah Daddy aint like using it—and Im da same way.

Its funny summa da shit U pick up from Yo parents dat stays
wit ya.

A lotta of it be fucked up tho.

And you carry dat shit into Ya relationships.

And another thang is a lotta St. Louis streets are too small.

It's not like Memphis where the wide avenues make for a better flow of cars.

St. Louis is jammed pack with cars looking for enuff street to drive on.

And that shit drove me krazy when I first relocated here years ago.

But now that Im used to it, I rarely think about it.

It makes it easier to follow a muthafucka tho. Thats a PLUS.

I especially like the South Side near the Jefferson & Cherokee District for that type-a-shit.

Its one of the main reason I located my office there.

The crammed-together streets and alleys are perfect for ducking into and hiding in...or doing deals.

Sonja rang me.

I got a feeling you on da way.

Yo feeling is rite, baby. I just got thru thinking on you.

Umph.

We both knew it was Inevitable I would fuck HER sooner or later.

I just had to figger out how we could fuck without it being Disuptive to the Status Quo.

Cuz you know usually when you fuck a FRIEND thangs kan go South and yall become the Worstest ENEMIES.

How far you out, Daddy?

Im cumming frum da office, so maybe autha 10–15 mins depending on traffick.

All right. Im waiting, baby.

Riteous, baby.

———

I putt mah mind back on meandering thru traffick.

I wanted to git mah shit from Sonja before I saw Abysinnia dats fa sho.

Sonja been growing her own various strains of weed for years now.

Like I said earlier tho, I onliest fuck wit regular weed.

She got them HEIRLOOM SEEDS I was able to git for her to grow dat regular weed.

See, cuz Ion fuck round wit none of this Weed they got outcheah now dat dont nobody know what da fuck is really goings ons wit it!

Ion smoke er'body weed just like I dont eat er'body potato salad. Heah me?!

The weed she grows for me still tastes like dat 70s Grass, U heah me?

Damn near kan taste the DIRT in it!

And the HIGH is beautiful wit none of that LSD effect U git from this hi-tech weed thats on da streets now.

That shit is twisting Niggaz minds up in all kinds of directions too.

But when you got the RITE kinda weed aint nuthing like a room full of good SMOKE and Pussy PHEROMONES.

Thats a helluva an ELIXIR just by itself.

And it takes me DEEP when I combine and INHALE em both at the rite time.

It takes the Woman who is involved in the ritual even DEEPER

Thats why I had sum koncern for Abysinna.

She aint never had this type of werk before.

And I done had a couple of Sistaz LOSE it during the process — and damn near never made it back....which is da kinda shit dat bothered me for way too long afterwards.

Yet, The WORK got done.

Butt I still aint never liked that.

Im all rite in mah spirit wit it.

I just promised mah self to avoid dat type-a-shit wherever possible.

Altho, to be fair to mah self, it happened when I was younger in This Game of Innerstanding How Pussy Werks.

Nowadays, mah Kinnection with Pussy is so Strong its why mah Reputation proceeds me outcheah in this world gone mad.

Before I knew it I was pulling up to Sonjas house in University City, a suburb of St. Louis.

I sat in the car a minute. I could see one of her Goons lookin out.

The House she lived in was Huge.

I got out.

In broad daylight I was a Nigga in a cranberry red suit.

I wanted to be noticed.

In the environment I ran in it was good to be noticed WHEN you wanted to be noticed.

By the time I got to the front door of the big, ass house — the door smoothed its way open.

Sonja appeared magically and hugged me.

She was dressed in a see-thru sheer white, dress.

Her pubic hairs were shaved and coiffed.

She whispered a Nastyism in mah ear.

And then moved automatically over to the bar in the room and fixed me a Smirnoff Vodka and Tonic.

No Ice.

Just the way I like it.

Whats the use putting ice in a drink thats already got Water in it? That just fucks it up.

What are you working on this evening, Daddy?

You ever heard of a Sista named Abysinnia?

Cant say I have. She the latest?

Yeah baby. And I Think her case may go deeper than usual. But you know I dont talk too much bout mah shit.

Sonja nodded.

Yeah, I know. Never hurts to ask tho. You never know what-a-Mutha-fucka will tell you if you ask em at the rite time and place.

This be true.

Sonja woman was always pushing the envelope.

I sipped mah drink.

She pointed and one of her Goons moved quickly and came back with a package.

Yo shit is in there.

I peeped inside — and it smelled good enuff to eat.

I tasted it.

What say ye? Sonja asked.

I say Ye got this shit smelling damn good!

You see I rolled one for U already.

I nodded in the affirmative.

She smiled.

Then said: You gotta go I know.

True.

I took one last sip of mah drink and set it down.

We hugged again.

One of these days, Daddy, I swear Im gone have you love me righteously.

One of these days, I probably will and be GLAD you let-a-Nigga git in dat Thang.

We Kissed (a little).

And then I was out and in the car heading back to mah office.

Abysinnia case was cumming to a close I just had to make sho during the Ritual I dosed her rite.

15

The ride back frum Sonja house was Beautiful cuz of the Weed she had laid on me.

Regular Weed is a dying breed in this thankless world of today.

Butt you kan find it in St Louis if you know where to LOOK.

And WHO to ask.

And I know BOTH.

Cuz Niggaz like me still be in touch wit a time when that Reggie (thats the Street name here in the Muddy City) was all you needed to git High.

I never fucked wit HEROIN or none of dat CRACK shit, either.

Altho I know plenty of mah Niggaz who did.

And dem Niggaz is long gone, too.

Both Heroin & Crack was sum shit the Government put out in the 70s (and 80s) to destroy black communities.

Trust me, this aint just no Conspiracy shit im telling ya.

Mah Niggatel runs deep in this country--and *Spiritual Wickedness is in High Places.*

Thats frum NIGGAMASTE 6:12 in The Ancient Book Holy Book of NIGGAMASTE.

That's da other Book I was telling U about earlier.

Well, I got da book as Payment for mah Services Frum a grateful Sheik I helped on dat New Orleans case.

Anyway, bottom line is, Amerikkka don't care Nuthing bout No Niggaz as a whole.

And they been tryna Kill us off for years.

BARRY WHITE bass heavy voice blew out mah radio as I started back to mah spot to git ready for this final round wit ABYSSINIA tomorrow.

Sirius was playing back-to-back BARRY for sum reason and I was caught up on sum old feelings about mah Baby Mama when, Lo n behold, She called Me.

She musta felt me thinking about her.

I see I need to be careful thinking about You cuz now here U is calling.

Is that Rite? You MISS Me?

Wit every Bullet so far.

It was an old joke between us that always made her laff.

After she caught her breath she got to the point.

I need a READING.

Told you I dont do dat for You no mo O.

I called her O....short for OSHUN.

You could do this for me, BABA. I need this. I wanna talk to my Father one more time and I promise You I wont ask You about it again.

She called me BABA...Swahili for Daddy.

She was referring to the werk I do TALKING TO THE DEAD.

Butt I had stopped doing that for people cuz:

#1 it was too Traumatic for most of em.

And number #2: Ion like speaking to DEAD Muthafuckaz.

Cuz to do it U gotta wake em up a lotta times.

They dont LIKE dat shit!!

And Number #3: O was hard-headed about Following the Information received.

Once She Questioned me about was it ME or her DADDY Talking (cuz she ain't wanna do what she was being Tole) I Knew then I was done wit Opening that PORTAL to access the Realm of The DEAD & UNLIVING for Her.

We been round n round bout this O. And I tole U to find
sumbody else.

Ain't nobody else as good as U, Baba. U know dat.

You shoulda thought bout dat B4 U ran off at da Mouf.

Whatttttt??!! All I was asking for was Oconfirmation.

Butt I was tired of O shit.

Like most peeple who FUCK UP and then Spin da Story to
try and FIT Their Fuck Up--She was doing da SAME thing.

And I wasn't tryna HEAR It.

Cuz its just Noise.

A Nigga flapping they Gums tryna convince U of sum shit.

Cant help ya O, I said.

REALLY, Baba? dats how U gone do Me?

That's how U Did Yo SELF, baby. Dont Blame da shit on Me.

Alrite.

Aight. Gotta Go.

Okay, Baba....

I heard her start to say sumpen else....Butt I hung up.

She didnt fuck up mah HIGH Tho.

That REGGIE still had a Nigga feeling good like He shood.

I turned mah attention back to Sirius.

And ARETHA was Sangin bout R-E-S-P-E-C-T.

I like when shit Line up like dat to teach-a-Nigga a lesson.

This thought crossed mah Mind: If You dont RESPECT Yo SELF dont EXPECT Nobody Else to R-E-S-P-E-C-T You. PERIODT.

I rode on on home thinking about how in bout 48 hours now I would be staring into ABYSSINIA high yella Pussy for sum FINAL answers.

16

Back in mah office.

I was now about 2 days away frum seeing Abysinnia again.

I started thinking bout what MADAME X had said bout da Nigga She described to me that she had seent Abysinnia wit.

It dawned on me that he sounded like a no good, lousy muthafucka I knew bout named GREASY.

And if it was Greasy that meant some DISAGREEABLE, Fake Afrikan sexual majick shit was goings ons.

Frum what I knew, the Nigga was especially good at doing His bogus shit with unsuspecting Sistaz like Abysinnia who were just cumming into the so-called Consciousness Community.

And even tho She whudden totally naive, Slick Niggaz like Greasy had a way of Worming into a Woman life.

Anyway, it was not the CONscious Community.

I called it the COONSCIOUSNESS Community.

Because most of the Muthafuckaz involved in it are Hypocrites (just like in churches) who are always looking for a Sucker to CON outta of their Money or they MINDS.

And this was the Game that Greasy--and Niggaz LIKE--him have been playing with women for quite-a-many years.

His trail of Confusion, Broken Hearts and Missing Pussies was long as a Country Mile--and wide as a City Block.

And the Nigga was Vindictive.

So I knew all about him butt hadnt had to deal with any of his bullshit.

Til NOW.

That is IF it was Him.

Abysinnia would lemme kno fo sho.

I putt sum calls out for the latest Niggatel on Greasy.

I hit mah Nigga Stovepipe on the landline.

His cell had barely rang when he picked up.

Rev, wassup?!

Stove, You ever heard of a Nigga named Greasy?

Yeah. He into that Sex Majick shit, rite?

Mah Nigga Stovepipe stayed on top of his Game.

Yeah dats Him. What else U know bout him?

I know he visits Afrika a lot. And Atlanta.

Hmmmm. What else?

Thats bout all I know off top, Rev. You want me to check him out sum more?

Yeah. Do that. Check dat Atlanta konnection out fo me, too. Git back to me n lemme know sumpen in a few hours.

Im on it.

Next I hit Madame.

Hey, Lover.

I think that Nigga You told me bout is a Nigga named GREASY.

Why have I heard dat name before?

Because he runs around fucking with dem Sista Circle types on that Black Magick Erotica shit--And whoever else he can find in the so-called Conscious Community.

Rite-e-e-e-e-e-e! Now that You say that I think I know at least a couple of Sistaz he done messed around with that he fucked over.

Thats the Nigga M.O. fo sho. So look, here's what I need you to do for me.

Lemme git a pen, Daddy. (seconds) Alrite, Im ready.

Call The Sandman and see what he knows. He knows the background on everybody.

Alrite, Daddy. Will do.

Preshate U to the Fullest.

And I preshate U 2 Lova.

Me and Madame ended many of our calls like that.

In full appreciation of each-um-other.

Meanwhile...

I turned mah attention to mah Bookcase and went back to DOCTOR SUN STAR Book: PUSS EYE THRU THE AGES.

Sumpen TOLE me Abysinnia had a tight-lipped ELEPHANT-Type of Pussy (since she was an Amazon).

Many Peeple don't know dat da SHAPE of da Pussy has a lot to do wit da Personality of a Woman.

Just like a Number in Numerology has a bearing on You as well.

This is why No two set of Pussies are alike (just like fingerprints).

I made sum notes, googled sum additional info.

I could feel mah self gitting into the Zone for what was to cum.

The Oils, the Smells, the Music....ALL of these thangs had to be just rite.

Its no different than when U gitting ready to make love and

U wanna set the rite Mood for the best type-a-fuckin possible.

Only in this Case it had to be not just not Nice But truly PRECISE!

My main concern was whether or not Abysinnia was emotionally STABLE & AVAILABLE enuff to handle the Stress of going as DEEP as she needed to in order to brang back her Pussy.

I still whudden 100% sho about this Woman.

17

_____

48-Hours later, The Nite was a FULL MOON--which was rite on time like I knew it would be.

I had tole Abysinnia to git to mah office about 8 o'clock that evening.

But sumpen tole me she would arrive earlier than expected.

I was rite.

She showed up an HOUR early.

She was looking finer and smoother than Silk.

In fact, ironically, thats what She had on underneath this long, floor-length shawl she wore into mah office: She was dressed in a multi-colored, sheer, Silk Kimono.

Straight outta sum Asian shit.

I wondered, briefly, if that was the influence of Madame X Sensuality class

I could see her large, yellow titties n thighs thru the Kimono.

Thats how see-thruable it was.

I put mah hand inside the pocket of the Ritual Robe I was wearing and put it on mah Dick to calm it down since it wanted to act Ig-nant.

This wasnt the time or the place.

Not YET at least.

Are You ready to do this, baby?

I aint never been more ready to do ANYTHING in my life, Daddy.

(I nodded)

I went over to mah bookcase, hit the button so the panel slid back.

Go on down them steps.

She walked past me--and I could smell her WETNESS.

I quieted the FREAK in me for the moment.

It aint too late to Change ya mind, ya know.

No, I want this, Daddy. I want it BAD.

I always keep asking up to the very last minute wit mah Wommins.

Yeah, I kan tell U want it badd. I just like to be SHO. Thats how I keep frum BOTH of us frum having a BAD EXPERIENCE.

I dont blame You. But I damn sure am not about to Miss this opportunity to help myself.

Thats why I likes You.

We both laffed, easing the tension that was building for what we knew was cumming.

I was liking Her more than I wanted to ADMIT to mah self.

––––––––

When I do mah Rituals I play lovemaking music.

That may seem weird to You.

Irregardless, I still need to set the same mood cuz Im gitting ready to have a Convo wit not only the Body of a deeply concerned Woman--but an Intimate dialogue with The Pussy Proper, too.

A conversation that could Make or Break Her.

I looked at Abysinnia and told her to GIT UNDRESSED.

She obeyed me as if She was Hypnotized--so I knew Her Mind, Body & Soul had already prepared itself for this undertaking.

She let the thin, silk Kimono slide from her body to the Flo.

The Yellow Lights that I used for these occasions hit Her Yellow Skin and had her body giving off an Angelic Glow.

She looked like she was standing in a Halo of Glory.

Her Pheromones were on HIGH and were reeking frum her every Orifice.

I could even smell her ASS.

The Freak in me loves the smell of a Womans ASS (especially when Im making love to a woman and the smell of the Cootchie mixes with the smell of the Booty....I call that scent: BOOTCHIE).

The BOOTCHIE was strong in here this nite.

I wish could BOTTLE that scent--and SELL it to muthafuckaz.

And one day I just MITE

Abysinnia stood NAKED before Me wit her hands by her side, looking VULNERABLE and EDIBLE at the same time.

I had the Ritual Table that I had inherited frum mah Daddy set up in the middle of the room.

It was made out of the softest lambskin leather in the world.

Mah Daddy had been given the table as a Gift for one of the cases he had solved years ago in Saudia Arabia. (yeah...we international wit this shit).

As Abysinnia walked over to the table she seemed to be moving in Slow Motion.

Her ass rippled & undulated, gently--as tho they were being swayed by an invisible breeze.

She approached the table and laid down smoothly like she had been practicing the moovements. (and who knows? Maybe she had to fuck with mah Mind....after all She was a natural born Witch--whether she knew it or not).

I walked to the corner and began playing OLIVIA (LOST & TURNED OUT) by The WHISPERS.

I still use old skool records cuz the Needle on the Vinyl is the safest, strongest and most effective Megahertz viberations when you do this work.

Cuz You always want the sounds that the music creates to be of the Highest Quality that goes in ya Ear Hole and hits Ya Ear Drum.

Its no different frum consuming food.

You ever heard of JUNK FOOD?

Well, there is such-a-thang as Junk MUSIC, too.

Therefore, what You consume and Digest in Ya EAR as Sound is JUST as important as what you consume and Digest in Ya Stomack.

———

Abysinnia stirred when she heard the music.

How did you know OLIVIA is one of my favorite songs in the world?

You already know, baby.

Right. Its A Gift.

She laid still again.

I could tell she was zoning in.

GOOD.

She was a Natural for this.

Her skin was GLISTENING as she lay LISTENING.

I could see I was gonna have to be careful wit this Woman cuz mah Feelings were growing.

And one of mah Hard, Fast Rules was: always Keep Mah FEELINGS out of the way of the HEALINGS.

Cuz its not about ME and what Mah DICK wants.

Its about The Woman and The Freedom of her LOINS.

Abysinnia and I had cum to that moment of No Return.

She had had her chance to not go Anutha Furtha.

Butt She CHOSE to open the portal We was about to Enter.

18

As Abysinnia laid perfectly still, except for her fluttering EYElashes
—I flashed back to an earlier Convo I had wit Stovepipe before
Abysinna showed up.

He had called back wit da Niggatel I had asked him to find
out on GREASY: Turns out, Sho nuff, This was da EXACT,
SAME Nigga Madame X had seen Abysinnia wit earlier.

Rev, you were rite about dat Nigga. He on dat fake Sex Majick shit.

Um-hm. What else?

Its just like U said. The Nigga done fucked up a bunch of Sistaz wit
dat sex game. AND: here the surprising part. The Nigga got a whole
crew running this Game.

Where we tom bout? ATLANTA?

Nah, he done slowed up on dat LOCATION.

Hmmm. So What we tom bout? How many Niggaz?

All His shit out da LOU now. Got maybe 6 or 7 of Niggaz as part of

His Crew. They got a old, big ass house on the southside. I heard its laid out on the inside tho.

Where at on the Southside?

Over by Carondelet Park.

They closer to the Water side where the lakes at or over by Main Road?

By the Water.

Umph....Now aint THAT sum shit?

I knew all bout Carondelet Park—and it made sense in a Warlord type-a-way since a lotta of St. Louis peeple of the Caucasion Persuasion liked using that Park for SORCERY ritualistic shit.

Butt over the years, a lotta Niggaz who was into this bogus bullshit Majick had started congregating around the Park, too.

Aight. And you SHO dat Nigga GREASY is da one Abysinnia got fucked up wit?

On EVERYTHING, Rev. I chased dat shit all da way down like you showed me how to do to where it cant be nobody BUT Him.

Solid. Preshate it, Stove.

Hey, Rev. Much as you done done for me, you know its all I kan do to help you wit Anythang Mah Nigga.

Digg dat. Keep ya eye on da Streets. Stay Vigilant.

Rev, I'm watching these streets like 5-0 looking to fuck wit a Nigga.

No dout.

I clicked off wit Stovepipe—and stood there holding mah phone in mah hand reflecting on what I knew all along about Niggaz like Greasy who were ALL OVER the so-called Conscious Community.

Like I said earlier, I call it the COONscious Community: cuz its just as full of Hypocrites, Charlatans, Perverts & Cons.

—and da Negroes involved in it aint no better than the fucked up Churches that many of em call they Self running away frum hoping to find sumpen better on the other side of Knowledge.

So true to form, Greasy nem all over the muthafucka running they Con Game—and katching Naive Sistaz who just be cumming into the Knowledge of Self—and who be looking to hook up wit a Real Nigga they THINK is on sum AUTHENTIC Higher Conscious shit.

And before You know it, them Niggaz been done SNATCHED Her ass into They program and have her HOOKED on all kinds of E-Vil and Ill-Advised SEXUAL DARK ARTS n shit.

I turned mah attention back to Abysinnia.

Her breasts were rising in gentle formation.

She was taking Shallow breaths.

BREATHE DEEPER, Abysinnia.

Mah voice seem to cum frum a different part of me and out thru mah mouf and into her ears.

She obeyed immediately and I watched her Stomach sink in as she took the deeper breath.

I had Olivia on repeat.

I stripped outta mah robe and oiled mah self with Virgin Coconut Oil.

I took Abysinnia hand—and placed a nice amount of the oil in her palm.

Go head to toe with this I instructed her.

People dont know that Virgin Coconut Oil is not just for sum of the DEEPEST, Sincerest Fucking known to Man because the Oil is nearly the same as the KALA FLUIDS in the Pussy—butt its also just the shit U want for warding off Unwanted entities that kan cum thru da Pores of Yo Skin.

Rub Yo self throughly.

Yes, Daddy.

Usually, I would rub the oil on The Client mah self.

Butt I didnt trust mah self rite now wit Abysinnia.

This was DIFFERENT on a whole notha level—especially, seeing as how she was involved wit-a-Nigga who was the foundation of a lotta shit that was RONG wit the Conscious Community.

Even mah Dick was behaving:

It wasnt Hard.

It was Chillin like a Villin.

Relaxed.

Like IT knew.

It DID know.

I got mah WEED stash I had got frum SONJA—and fired up a big, ass BLUNT.

Then, I lit sum MARIJUANA INCENSE that wasnt on the market yet.

I know you thinking: CANNABIS INCENSE??!!

Yeah, thats rite cuz in mah line of work Im tapped into all kinds of legal and Illegal shit that I may or MAY not use to help-a-Nigga outta bad SHITuation.

On the other hand, I dont fuck wit burning incense in general tho—cuz thats sum muthafuckin toxic fumistic shit —that NOBODY should be inhaling in an enclosed space.

Cuz the Colored Dyes in most of this Incense thats outcheah Is OUTLAWED in most other Countries EXCEPT Amerikkka.

And Niggaz INHALING that shit on the regular—not realizing they fucking they Chromosomes up.

I aint preaching tho.

Im just WARNING.

I turned the volume up frum 6 to 9 on mah old skool Technics turntable just as The Whispers sang the words: *LOST AND TURNED OUT-T-T-T-T!!*

The room was WHITE wit Incense Fumes & Blunt Smoke.

Here take a hit I told her.

I handed her the Blunt—and She hit it HARD n LONG.

I had to gently force the blunt outta her hand to keep her frum dragging even deeper.

She WANTED THIS.

She broke out in a light SWEAT.

She began to speak in Tongues— so I knew she was going under The Smoke.

I understood every word she was saying.

The language of KINARTOOROO.

Its the language of TONGUES.

Her body began to move on the large table as tho she was involved in the sexual act—and I KNEW it was time.

I watched Her for about 5 minutes because ONE it was EROTIC—and TWO and more importantly: I was studying her Body Language.

Most of the shit we cummunicate to one another is Silent, ya digg?

Peeple have no idea the amount of words THEY are

Cummunicating without them even OPENING They MOUF.

Thats why 5 minutes is all I need wit most Folks to tell if They ain't bout shit.

The way Abysinnia was mooving now made me start questioning her Out Loud:

19

Do you understand that ALL yo answers must be
TRUTHFUL to the Utmost?

I walked around the room, breathing deeply to take in all
the Blunt smoke that was circulating round da room.

Whole time I was speaking to Abysinna.

She didnt know that I had found out dat it was Greasy who
she had been Fuckin wit and hoo had Fucked her over.

Yes, Daddy. All I want is The TRUTH.

Butt thats not what You get is it?

*No. Only my Mama. I can talk to Her about ANTHING. And I kan
trust her to tell me EVERYTHING. She always keeps it straight
with Me.*

What would Yo Mama say about YOU?

That I'm Stubborn like my Daddy.

And What bout Yo Daddy? Yall Kool too?

I was Probing to build that Trust I know she didden give easily to a Muthafucka.

She aint say nuthing for a minute tho.

Then:

We useta git along perfectly fine— and then we fell out when I was in highschool. Butt Im still krazy about my Father.

Indeed. I understood this—at the same time I know Many Men hoo dont.

See, what a lotta us Men Folk dont understand is that a lotta times a Womans DADDY is The FIRST Man to BREAK Her heart—and MANY of them never recover from dat shit.

I done had to help a quite-a-many Sistaz git back They entire SPIRIT let-a-lone The ESSENCE of they MONEY MAKER—after being raised in a house where they was having regular Falling Outs with They Daddy—or where the Daddy had been forced to be ABSENT for reason or another.

So when I heard Abyssina say what she said bout HER Daddy—I wasn't serprized at all.

Understand Me this: Finding out a Woman relationship wit Her Daddy is Krucial to Innerstanding summa da shit she going thru in her Current SHITuationshp also known as a RELATIONSHP wit-a-Nigga.

Many-A-Nigga wit Bad Intentions will exploit and SEXploit a Woman knowing this shit.

Butt wit Me, I Putt dat On EVERY THANG, dat even wit da POWERS I'm werking wit, I ain't NEVER been into dat type-a-shit.

And truth be tole: never had a mind to.

Then again—Most Niggaz ain't got a CLUE no how.

And they dont Want one.

Cuz The Hookup Game is Treacherous outcheah now.

Its a Battle of da Sexes goings Ons between Black Mens and Wommins.

I saw tears start to run down Abysinnia face.

So no doubt it was a sensitive subject for her.

Are you still in touch wit ya Daddy?

We talk here and there. But he still dont approve of my life.

And what type of life is that?

(I KNEW cuz she had tole me earlier. Butt I just wanted to hear her say it out rite again now that we had began the Ritual).

Polygamy and Polyamory. He knows Im into having Multiple Men as Lovers--or Men who have more than One Wife.

Um-Hm. And there we go. Rite up a Born Insecure Nigga like Greasy's alley.

That Polygamy game is his thang.

Whats fucked up about it is that Polygamy useta be this true kinda Holy Matrimony back in the day.

You kan tell that MARRIAGE is actually based on the Woman just by that Word: MATRIMONY. M-A-T is for the MATRIX and the Matrix is for the MAMA or MOTHER.

All Unions are meant to PRESERVE the Woman—butt only if a Nigga DESERVE-a-Woman, ya digg??

Why is dat U ask?

Because Ancient Niggaz who came way before US all knew that The WOMAN is One of the most PRECIOUS FAMILY JEWELS in the CROWN of Hueman existence—and must be Protected in all places and spaces til death do yall part.

We caint ever forgit that the Journey of EVERY Nigga who cums frum the LIGHT—and into the World—may START in a Nigga NUTS--butt ENDS in the WOMB of The WOMAN, ya understand??

Therefore a woman must CHOOSE carefully Hoo her Reproductive System gits ALIGNED with.

In other words: The Woman ALWAYS Keeps The RIGHT To CHOOSE.

Most men dont even realize that THEY are da ONE who is being CHOSEN cuz they THINK they are the one doing the CHOOSING.

This is a process that been KORRUPTED in the world we live in Today.

Thats why Personally, because of the Krucial n Kritical Nature of Relationships that hang in such-a-balance in the modern society, I fucks for KEEPS or not at all.

The table was made in such a way at the far end that I could part ABYSINNA big, naked, yellow Thighs.

I turned the music all the way down.

And walked up between her large Gams.

Abysinnia was moving her body again.

Very slow—like a Snake.

I knew those moves on an Intimate level...Not wit her, ya understand??

Butt I knew they were the familiar motions meant for MATING.

She was in the Spirit and in the Moment dat was bout to CUM.

She started up autha stream of speaking in Tongues.

I let her flow and stored her words to memory for later in the session.

I sat on a seat that I had made n reserved for these exact occasions.

Her Pubic Mound Sat Up like it was on a Sacred Hill.

Her CLIT was large and engorged—yet, it was laid back in its HOOD. I always said the Clit Lives in da Hood butt I aint never been afraid to go there.

Beads of sweat ran from her Pussy and down the lower, inner folds of her Vulva.

I tasted it wit one of mah index Finga—and it confirmed
mah thoughts: she was within 10 days of Menses.

Then:

Once again, I started the process that had made me world
famous.

I begin to HUM to The PUSS EYE.

Mah Song had started because I was about to learn the
Secrets of Abysinnia's Honeypot.

20

Mah humming made Absynnia TWITCH in anticipation of further questioning.

I swear fo da Niggod in Me this woman had summa da STRONGEST Hormonal SCENTS & SECRETIONS in the known world.

Her personal Smells cumming frum tween her Thighs was So strong and pungent I could TASTE It drippin down mah wet Throat.

And it was mixing wit the faint Fumes of the Cannabis Incense I had burning—and that shit was making an Erotic Aroma.

I made a skull note to mix it as a Formula for future rituals going forward cuz I knew dat would be sum powful shit.

I took a long drag on the Blunt and blew the smoke towards Abysinnia's Vagina.

HARMONY cum forth!

I called Her PUSSY by Name.

Abysinnia raised her delicious-smelling ass off the table in a WIGGLE to meet the sound of mah Deep voice.

She spread her leggs wide to receive the Vibration.

And Her luscious CLIT was in mah Face like sum one was pushing a purrty, giant Button into mah Face.

The Foreign Tongue that came outta mah Mouf was one I knew that HARMONY would know.

Again: It was the Language called KINARTOOROO, the tongue Abysinnia had been speaking unconsciously--I was now speeking on Purpose.

It was second nature for me.

And it was One of the rarest arts still practiced by Niggaz like ME who had been Born to do this work of talking To THE PUSS EYE.

Abysinnia Stirred her Hips as I kept calling Harmonys Name.

Her big button of a CLIT started Trembling--and Unfolding.

I just watched it cuz I knew what was happening.

If U have ever seen a Flower BLOOM in slo-motion then U know what its like to see a Womans Clitoris gain Consciousness.

Which meant the Pussy was becumming awake to the Frequency of mah Strong Intonations.

Unfortunately, Most Niggaz go rite to the Clitoris cuz they think its main purpose is for PLEAZURE.

And this is where they Fuck Up.

If U really knew then U would know the Clitoris is the Symbol that connects to the PINEAL GLAND cuz its the GATEWAY to a Womans SUBCONSCIOUSNESS.

Indeed, the THIRD EYE is The PUSS EYE.

As a sweet, white nectar oozed from her Clit, I could see that Abysinnia was ready to go deeper.

She SPOKE—butt Her VOICE had Changed to a LOWER octave—and I knew it was Not HER butt HARMONY that had finally cum into the Present Moment.

Why Am I Here?

The PUSSY was speaking thru Abysinnia.

Because WE need Answers....or better yet: The Body You LIVE IN Needs Answers about why You Left.

I NEVER Left. I just became QUIET.

I had heard this reasoning before.

And Innerstood it.

But Your Solitude has caused a Crisis in the Body you occupy. At a time when YOU are MOST needed.

The Crisis is one of Consciousness that SHE has not Heeded. And if

Her lack of Awareness endangers US Both I have no Choice butt to Shut Down all Feelings and Emotions. Or ELSE.

Or Else WHAT?

There was No Answer from Harmony.

Butt the Point was Clear.

KNOW THIS: Every sexual act that we engage in is Written upon our LOINS that will carry the story of The Encounter for its Life Time.

The Depth and Trauma or GOODNESS of that Story will be shared with Every One we Make Love With because its Etched into our DNA.

In other words: Fucking out of ALIGNMENT has sum Serious Repercussions.

What Do I Mean?

I mean Gitting Down wit-a-Nigga thats NOT on Yo Frequency.

That shit Kan and WILL cum back on You.

HARD.

Oh, you may enjoy dat NUT or ORGASM You git at the time, ya digg?

(because the NERVOUS SYSTEM dont give a Fuck about what DRUG turns it ON).

But Yo WHOLE SOUL (and Especially a Womans HOLE SOUL) Will FLIP-da-Fuck Out.

I aint make the RULES.

Im just TELLING You about em.

And I aint Preaching.

Im just Teaching.

And Abysinnia had stumbled head first (literally) into a SHITuation wit GREASY that had shut down her Lower Chakra.

———

I addressed HARMONY again.

Im only seeking to loose her from The BIND U have on her.

No, She is the One who must loose ME. I AM only protecting Whats Rightfully OURS.

And WHAT must She Do?

BANISH Her Feelings from the current Situation that has ensnared Her.

Butt she does not have COGNIZANCE of This.

In her HEART She Does.

So She needs to have a Heart-to-Heart WIT her Heart? Why not You?

As soon as I asked the question I Immediately knew the ANSWER:

Because Abysinnia had made a Cardinal Mistake that many Women make. She had given her HEART without Consulting Her PUSSY!

Harmony continued to Flow:

I, like Many who hold this Position in the body of A Woman, are often left out of the Love Equation when She CUMS. Even tho when She CUMS we have Beared (and Shared) the Responsibility. She cant lay this BURDEN Down until She lays this Relationship DOWN.

I listened.

Only then can I Restore myself to Her—and NOT before that time.

I made anutha skull note to remember that No Pussy kan CUM back before its Time.

Harmony got real quiet after that.

21

The way Abysinnia was slightly shaking I could tell that small orgasms were running thru her.

GOOD.

Cuz that meant She was going deeper into the moment.

Exactly what I wanted.

I aint want no Blocks on her Mental.

I broke into Abysinnia's Channeling--and spoke directly to her now.

Abysinnia who is GREASY?

She was Groggy wit Sexual Innergy and answered slowly.

You know about Greasy? She purred the question.

Yes. I do.

He is the Brother Im seeing—but I want to STOP seeing.

Why dont You?

Im trying—but I keep going Back to him.

Are you hip to the Majick he fucks around wit?

Yes. I Am. Thats one of the reasons I began seeing him in the first place.

Then You must be hip to why thats one of the reasons you are also trapped wit da Nigga.

Abysinnia seemed caught off Guard.

I didnt think about that.

Many wommin never do when they think the Nigga is Legitimate.

I mean, I never thought that Sex could have that kinda Affect.

Fucking is NEVER without Consequences--be they good or bad.

So You are saying I have been Caught Up?

TRAPPED is more like it.

Why would he want to ENTRAP Me?

Some peeple Pray FOR Muthafuckaz--and sum Peeple PREY "On" Muthafuckaz. Kan U Digg it? And Niggaz like Greasy always need a Victim to do what they WANT them to do. And In YO case He needs You to help Catch other Wommin coming into that world of Sex Majick.

Abysinnia was QUIET.

Her disappointment spoke Volumes.

But I continued droppin.

You know I have been speaking wit HARMONY during this session, rite?

Yes. I could hear HER but I couldnt Interrupt or Kontrol Her.

I nodded.

The PUSSY is very often out of Kontrol. For BETTER or WORSE as the case may be. And thats as its supposed to be. I trust You, Abysinnia--However, at a time like this, I trust Yo Pussy even more for the unaulterated truth.

And what have you learned?

That You have taken on much of the KARMIC PAYBACK meant for Greasy.

How so?

You slept with Him—and he CAME inside You, rite?

Yes. I did. Because I believed in the Majick.

Both a woman AND her Pocketbook kan be an Open Portal during such times—which kan be a fucked up outcum with the wrong Muthafucka.

I was looking for something DIFFERENT in mah Life.

You was Looking—butt You wasnt THINKING, baby, ya digg?

So you are saying I've taken on Karma Meant for HIM instead?

Basikally. And so Has Harmony.

Abysinnia was stunned into further silence.

Like many wommin She was Smart yet Dumb about the Ways of The Pussy She Owned.

And actually, its no different for Us Menfolk, too.

We have a DICK butt we dont KNOW The Dick we carry between our Thighs.

Listen to me Abysinnia. What U must never forgit after this is that KARMA Is Also a SEXUALLY TRANSMITTED DISEASE.

Wow, Daddy!!!! I dont know what to say.

She was still speaking groggily.

But Awareness was setting in.

Sexually Transmitted Karma?! I have never heard of that in my life!

Its REAL in the FEEL, baby. I understand that. BUTT: there are a lotta muthafuckaz walking round rite now carrying TROUBLES and PROBLEMS that were passed to them when they SLEPT with Someone UN-DESERVING of the access to they Body—or even worse someone who was actually TRYNA pass on the Karmic Debt so they wouldnt have to suffer by themselves. And now that SUM ONE is You!

You think GREASY would do that?!

NO.

You dont?

No. I dont Think. I KNOW He da type-a-Nigga who would do that.

Abysinnia lay still as a corpse—butt her Thoughts were mooving at 1,000 miles per hour.

Then: I thought I was in LOVE with Greasy in sum kinda way, Daddy. I must admit that I allowed him to tap into a part of Me I had let Sleep.

I could see that parts of her Mind didnt wanna give up on What she was feeling for Greasy—DESPITE what he had done--and this is often the HARDEST part of what I Do wit a Woman and Her JEWEL.

You know what the Thang bout LOVE Is?

No, what's That, Daddy?

Its sum IRRATIONAL SHIT. And if You wanna FREE Yo Mental and HARMONY You gotta return to RATIONALITY.

And how do I do that, Daddy?

Lay Still a minute while I align with Harmony one mo time.

22

I knew Abysinnia Pussy was on the verge of NEVER
returning to her--and that shit had me a just a lil bit Uneasy.

Because Iike I said: I HATE losing a Pussy.

And worse, I hate losing the Woman. Cuz if U lose the
Pussy the Woman is lost too.

SEXUAL fragrance was all in the air (and in mah Nose) as I
took a moment to think how to address Harmony one mo
again.

We were at a crossroads in this ritual.

Abysinnia was tryna hold on to what She THOUGHT She
had while Harmony was tryna achieve Balance between Her
Thighs.

I looked over in the corner where I kept mah Djembe, an
african drum.

And I knew it was time to Beat it.

I only played it for Emergencies.

And now this was one.

Cuz I knew when I played the Djembe it meant that I would have to go DEEPER mahself to unbind Absyinnia spirit loose frum Greasy.

And this meant taking an Out-of-Body journey to the Center of her Vaginal portals via mah Mind--which meant literally taking mah CONSCIOUSNESS and putting it DEEP in her Pussy to engage the Entity that was lodged there by Greasy.

Because thats where KARMA in the form of a spiritual entity resides in a BODY.

Especially, the Body of a Woman.

Because Women are VESSELS of Containment during the Sexual Act.

And if they are not kareful WILL be and KAN be the Recipient of all kinds of Bad Shit cumming frum a Nigga they giving themselves, too.

Many dont understand this--and how it works.

And NEVER will, Unfortunately.

And still others dont even believe shit like this is REAL: that fucking is sum highly Spiritual (CONTAGIOUS) shit!

23

I took off mah robe and mah 12-inch PENIS stuck straight out.

Yes, Im BLESSED & HIGHLY-FAVORED in dat Regards butt I use Mah DICK for GOOD and Not E-VIL to tickle the Wombs and Cervixes of sertain kinds of Wommin Folk.

Its throbbin n bobbin head was inches away frum Abysinnia's nice, tight Orifice.

I could tell it was tight just by eye-balling it cuz its what I do.

But this wasnt about to be that.

This was about Me stripping for complete access for this special type-a-ritual.

I had to be completely NAKED and OPEN.

All PORES open and ready to the spiritual entities that were already in the room and just waiting for this moment.

So yes, mah DICK was harder-than-CHINESE ARITH-
METIC for the occassion.

Butt when U start to Innerstand SEXUAL INNERGY on a
Majician's level U cum to know that not all Sexual Arouse-
ment is meant to begin or end in Fucking.

Its meant to be the start of Dislodging an Un-Natural Spirit
frum the Presence of YOU and YOURS--or in this Case to
BANISH a Counterfeit Spirit frum a Woman's LOVE BOX.

Or Absorb the Same frum a MAN (as Madame X often does
during her work with the flipside wit the PENIS).

I Oiled mahself in the finest Virgin Coconut Oil in the world
that I kept hidden for these moments.

I gave Abysinnia anutha hit on the Blunt--and began playing
the Drum.

I was playing the riddim specifically meant to raise the Love
Vibration in the room.

I knew the effect it would have.

She started Moaning, loudly.

So I knew in her mind She was fucking--and I could see that
the way her body was wriggling on the table that she was
fucking too.

Truth be tole: I was the One who was Fucking her because
this was a True MIND FUCK.

Folks use dat word tho without knowing what a REAL
one is.

I kept up the Riddim: Mind Fucking her slow but sho.

Whats happening to me, Daddy? This feels so Goooood!

Just relax baby. I got U. We gotta go sumwhere. You, Me and Harmony.

Where we going, Daddy?

We going DEEP, Lover.

I called her LOVER for this moment because thats what She needed to BE and FEEL without question for this sexual exploration of the Spiritual Kind of the Mind.

Mah hands were making that Drum sang its song.

Absyinnia was Moaning very loud but low like a Lioness in heat.

It was sum GUTTERAL shit I rarely heard.

And THEN:

HARMONY came thru to me, speaking intensely.

You are trying to go where No Man is supposed to Go unless they deserve to be there.

I Do.

You are not to go that far in this Woman who is already in krucial conflict about herself.

I Am only trying to Retrieve and Entity that both YOU and HER are having a hard time Un-Binding.

She only has to let go.

But she Cant because of her Mental State.

Then I have no Choice but to remain as a BLOCK to this kinda Violation.

I bow to Your Wizdom, HARMONY. Im only here at HER request to Assist You in bringing her back to Rejoin You in such-a-way that you both kan be at Peace once again. Kan U allow me to help with this ELEVATION rather than a VIOLATION?

Thats Rite.

I was speeking Game, yall, at the PUSS EYE of Absynnia almost in desperation which I usually never do.

Butt I kared bout her in a way I dont normally do wit Wommin.

Sumhow I knew what I was doing was gitting her ready for ME.

This was a Test.

And truth be tole I was gitting Doubtful.

She had a Strong and Determined PUSSY who knew how to Protect her.

And it was determined that she DIE INSIDE first before it would let her be Absorbed into anutha Detrimental situation.

I had never seen a Pussy wit such an Attitude as this.

This is how I knew Abysinna and I were meant to work 2gether in sum kinda way.

Sexual or Not.

So I kept rapping hard to persuade Harmony.

Will U allow me to do this? I repeated.

If I let U doo this WUT happens 2 Her Spirit?

She will be kool. And dats mah werd. I have neva lost a Pussy or a Soul as long as I have been dooing this.

Butt there is always a chance rite?

True-I nodded. Butt the chances of her neva recovering frum the shit she has been thru is even greater if we DONT doo this.

Harmony thawt a long moment.

Then:

Alright. I will step aside with that understanding as my vibration and do all I kan to assist you.

Inside I was amped I had made sense to Harmony.

I stood up between Absyinnia's beautiful, glistening thighs, as she continued making low, beastly sounds.

She was in what I called The JUNGLE moment.

A Deeply sexual mood that a Woman should never allow

herself to go to Unless that NIGGA is most definitely
THE ONE.

I kept mah Penis inches away frum her OPENING—and
then slid deep into the BACK of Harmony.

But it was only in Mah MIND—and HER Mental.

Maintaining contact wit the Mind of Absyinnia and traveling
spiritually into the Back of Harmony was what I had to do to
if I was gonna be able to Save her.

It was Now or Never.

It was git rite or git left.

And I wasnt BOUT to lose this Woman.

24

The Danger of entering a Woman's Mind who is feeling sum Kind of way bout-a-Nigga is that U kan git TRAPPED in the recesses of her SYNAPSES and NEURONAL KONNECTIONS.

But You DO it if She WORTH it.

And Abysinnia was damn sho worth it to me.

I could see that more than I cared to admit to anybody.

Of course, I had to let The PUSSY know.

Thats really what made her gone head and lemme do this work wit Abysinnia.

She could see I was really caring bout Abysinnia.

Said The PUSSY:

If You LOSE Her You Lose US Both.

Im Aware of that which is why I dont plan on Losing neither one of You.

Many plans never cum to Fruition.

This one will.

I kept re-assuring Abysinnia's Pussy as we engaged in a intense convo about her Owner's safety.

As I said, in the end I won HARMONY over to mah way of thinking.

Then, let us proceed said Harmony. What am I to do?

Be very STILL and concentrate on being ONE wit Me as I go in.

———

Naked as da day I was born, I began walkin round da room Whispering Abysinna name.

She had never stopped stirring on the table as I talked to her Sweet Spot.

And now, once again, she was Moaning n Groaning in Low ecstasy.

Gimme Yo Mind Abysinnia, I Whispered intently. Gimme Yo mind guh.

Huh, Daddy? She asked in a low voice.

Open Yo Mind to me.

She was in a deep trance and responding slowly.

Im SCARED, Daddy. Ion know how to feel or deal rite now.

Its gone be kool, baby. U gotta trust me.

She Sat Up wit her eyes closed real tight.

Can U hold Me, Daddy?

I approached Abysinna and turned sideways so Mah long, hard Dick would not Poke her in the Stomack and—held her in a firm squeeze.

I could feel her heart beating as she Relaxed into me.

Is this gonna hurt, Daddy?

Nah, baby. Its gonna HELP. Now gone n lay back down.

As I released mah grip she laid back on the table and I grabbed her ankles and spread her legs.

Harmony was facing straight ahead.

I pushed her legs back towards her head.

You woulda thawt we were gitting ready to fuck butt—of course, we whudden .

Butt going deep like this often calls for the same type of Motions as tho you WAS gitting ready to fuck.

I needed HARMONY staring me straight in the face.

Her PHEROMONES were on fire and off the chart even more now!!

I took a deep a breath and inhaled her Musk as deep into mah lungs as I could.

Think on me and why Im here to help U.

Yes, Daddy.

Abysinnia was being Obedient which was a krucial first step in this journey to return her and Her Pussy to BALANCE.

I sat between her legs once mo and began chanting directly into Harmony.

Her Puss Eye was GLISTENING (and LISTENING).

It was a Sexy moment but not in the way of gitting ready to Fuck.

But in the way of branging up the Sexual Innergy known as Kundalini.

Kundalini is that Innergy that resembles the shape of a SNAKE as it crawls up Yo spine when you and ya lover start gitting ready to git down in dem sheets.

You git Hard and SHE gits WET.

Both yall be drippin Pre-Cum.

25

Abysinnia went frum DRIPPIN to LEAKING which was as it shood d be the further She got in.

The Work I do is best done at the highest levels of FUCK-ING-MINDED Thoughts.

There should be no Difference.

And there AINT gone be no difference as long as Im on The Case.

All PUSSIES are konnected to the VAGUS NERVE.

Knowing this is NITE and DAY in how a Nigga approaches the PUSS EYE.

The Sacral-Sacred Area known as the G-SPOT is the GOD-SPOT konnected to that Vagus Nerve, ya see.

That VAGUS NERVE is the DIVINE Nerve that holds the Divinity of all Sexual Vibrations that go on in the body.

And this is what I knew bout Abysinnia:

Her Pussy was exceptionally Konnected to the Vagus Nerve Center, deep in the BACK of her Love Canal.

Which meant I was going to have to do sumpen I usually DIDNT have to do.

The times I done had to do it have been far and IN between.

Butt now with Abysinnia PUSSY damn near BEGGING me to go further and offer her Owner release I knew I was gonna have to: MASSAGE Abysinnia Vagus Nerve thru what I knew was bout to be a Hell of a SHAMANIC JOURNEY.

For in this way I would have a better and Ultimate kontrol of her Body in case thangs start gitting a lil too INTENSE.

26

A SHAMANIC JOURNEY is a Deeply involved Spiritual Quest in which I leave MAH Body and send mah CONSCIOUSNESS inside of whatever Vehicle or OTHER Body I need to go in.

True, for me, usually its a PUSSY or said anutha way: The MIND of the Pussy as well as The Body proper of the Woman at hand.

And now, I was inside of Abysinna.

Know this: you kan leave Yo BODY and cum back to it at a later date and time by just using your Mind and the high ancient, art Discipline of Hocus FOCUS.

This discipline requires a deep understanding of EYE-MAGINATION and Virtual Reality.

So as I sat in front of Abysinna, drumming, mah SPIRIT left mah BODY and Journeyed to the Inside of her Puss Eye PROPER.

She was in a Deep Trance and the inside of her Vagina was

139

Pulsating at a feverish pace as she moaned lightly, continuing to moove like a withering snake.

I immediately determined that I would need to go about 36-48 inches to submerge mah self in her nether regions to find the CURSE that was lodged deep in Her Vagina.

It was the only way I had any chance of helping her HEAL the VOID.

Abysinnia was almost mumbling her werds to me:

I dont know I guess just....in my desire to be in Harmony with Greasy, literally and figuratively--I got away from REASONING.

She was rite.

It Happens to the best of Us when we WANT something for THEM badder than we Want IT for ourselves.

This often puts us in HARMS Way of KARMA that cums to Visit upon the Other Person who is due for the Lesson.

And so, we too, will get that Work KARMA is about to pay to that ass.

27

As I went deep into the PUSS EYE of ABYSINNIA the PUSS EYE itself made room for me within its DEEPER Folds.

And I took mah Mind as far back into Abysinnia Pussy as I could manage.

It was a Fantastic Vaginal Voyage into the Deeper CENTER of the Puss Eye.

Strangely enuff, the further I delved into Abysinna vagina the more Counterfeit Spirits I encountered.

I was running into the GHOSTS of DEAD SPERM inside Abysinnia frum various Niggaz she had allowed to CUM inside her who werent deserving.

I could see that she had experienced and was holding onto an abundant level of PSYCHICAL TRAUMA within her FOLDS.

Many Wommin and Men dont realize that ANY TIME You have sex with sumbody they leave their Karma upon you and IN you!

Even when HUGGING peeple we have to be kareful.

The many Expressions of Affection that society have taught
US to do are actually not good such as Hugging complete
strangers or peeple U do not know.

U have to be kareful who U brang into your AURA.

And Wommin, ESPECIALLY, have to be kareful about who
She brangs into DA PUSS EYE!!

Because the Pussy is The TEMPLE only for The FAMILIAR
and The KNOWN....and as such is a SACRED (and Sacral)
GROUND that holds on to The ESSENCE of those who
Cum BEFORE It and IN It.

And this process must not be VIOLATED or The Woman,
Herself, Risks an Sextreme DANGER of Short-Circuiting
her own Spriritual Stability!!!!

And as I have said earlier: many Wommins never RECOVER
frum this, literally Dying on the Inside and often follow by
Physical Death within a matter of Years.

At a minimum her Personal spirit goes dormant and many
never even SPEEK again.

Its as tho she is the Walking Dead.

Its that Traumatic and Serious.

28

————————

Back inside Abysinnia: I grabbed hold of the GHOSTS of the DEAD NIGGA SPERM, snatching and releasing them one by one.

There were many so I knew Abysinnia I had been sexually active way above where She should have been in her younger life.

And I had never asked her how many Niggaz she had BODIED because thats sumpen I prefer a Woman to Voluntarily tell me.

Nevertheless, I was now finding out.

I wasnt judging her.

In fack, I was feeling sum kinda sorrow for her because she like many wommin dont understand the Depth of how Too Many DICKS kan KILL a womans Essence.

As I snatched and released the Counterfeit Spirits I kept looking for the most troublesome One of all that was bearing upon Her and Her PUSSY--the one belonging to the Nigga she had been dealing with: GREASY.

At last, I fount it and Addressed it on Abysinnia behalf:

You must cum out of this Pussy and return frum whence You came.

It was stubborn.

I do not wish to return frum whence I came. This is the place I am most comfortable at now.

Butt You are DRAINING this ENTITY. This Body Beautiful. And this is not good not for her.

Draining this Innergy is how I am able to stay alive.

Which is was true as all Counterfeit Spirits MUST do in order to Survive.

They make the HOST body their Domain to Remain in line with their Vampiric nature.

Still: I continued to dialogue with the Entity to git it to leave peacefully.

Because if it didnt I still had another trick up my Shaft to totally eliminate it.

I spoke to the Entity again:

Butt if SHE dies then U Die.

Then, that is how it must be. Why should I leave and DIE while SHE lives on without Me?

Because that was her life BEFORE You--and she deserves that honor once again.

She invited Me in--and I dont go where Im not welcum.

She invited YOU in under false pretences and frum Sum One she was accessible to.

We Wrestled with words and lexicon and as I could see that THAT wasnt working I began The SACRAL CHANT.

A Sacral Chant is the last resort for any LODGED Spirit inside a woman--and it ALWAYS works--except the Risk of Losing the woman increases due to the Massive Orgasms she will incur frum effort going on within her.

Butt it was all that was left to do if I Absyinnia was to have any chance of Returning to Groundation.

My CHANTING at the rite frequency began to take its hold on Abysinnia.

The Temperature in The Pussy heated up way past 120 Degrees at the CORE which assured me that Abysinnia could be a GREAT HOE if she wanted to because onliest the Wommins with the Potential for their Pussies to exceed 120 Degrees at the CORE under Hypnosis kan work at such a High Level.

Back deep in the Pussy: The Entity that had cum frum GREASY fought hard Butt so did I.

Abysinnia started having a HUMONGOUS ORGASM as The Entity and I went back and forth.

Her Vaginal Walls pulsated, popped and closed.

It was tho they too were werking to expel the THING.

Finally, when the Entity could no longer hold on it began to WITHDRAW from the Pussy Proper.

It was only then that I started backing out slowly of Abysinnia with mah Mind.

However, I was under pressure because just as I figgered, The Insane CUMMING Abysinnia was experiencing was Threatening to enclose mah Spirit Body within her before I was fully WITHDRAWN!

Moments like this kan be dangerous when U are out of yo body and deep inside the Pussy of a Woman.

But I had prepared for this and as she continued to Massively NUT and TREMBLE with CONNIPTIONS her Juices washed over mah Mental I rode the Flow of her Tides backwards and OUT of Her.

By the time I had reached Safely outside of her again--She was crying UN-CONTROLLABLY!!!!

And I LET Her.

29

Many peeple dont understand that TEARS--whether they be of Joy or SADNESS or CLEANSING to the WHOLE/HOLE/SOUL.

Thus, its important to NEVER stop a Person frum CRYING!!

Because often what is being CRIED OUT is the VERY thang that needs to leave them!!

So as the Tears RACKED her Mind, Body and (HOLE) Soul--and the INJECTION that had cum frum GREASY finished its Departure--I simply Watched--and Relaxed and became ONE with Her final dissolution.

We had Done it.

SHE had done it really.

I was just The PROCESS of Facilitation and Recuperation.

The Entity rolled thru her and OUT of Her and I SAW it do so.

Then, I knew Abysinnia was cumming back to herself and her PUSSY wood once again be ALIVE and Returned Unto Her.

30

I was just about to have a nutritious Breakfast Blunt when mah cell rang--and I could see it was MADAME X calling.

Sup Mama?

Madame loved when I called her by that name.

She was Mama and I was Daddy and dat shit jes GOES 2getha she always said.

Daddy?

Yeah-baby.

Just following up wit U like U tole me to.

I had arranged for Abysinnia to go thru a Healing and Retunement Ritual wit MADAME X that would help restore her entire Equilibirum to normality.

Talk to Me. HOW is erry Thang now wit Abysinnia?

Good as fuck.

Aw yeah?

Yes! In fact-BETTER than Good. Its GREAT. She has never been more connected to her Pussy than she is now. I think she finally understands what it means to actually HAVE One.

Thats DEEP-baby.

Well-its Thanks to YOU- daddy.

You know I do what I kan-Mama.

Truuuuuuue.

She stretched the word out almost like a song.

Then she said abruptly:

Kan I ask You something important-Daddy?

Yeah when U cum over this evenin-baby.

Ion kno why butt lissening to Madame on the phone had mah Loins ACHING to be in Her presence.

And jes by the way she asked me the question I knew she was feeling da same.

Umph-she said.

Then laffed dat soulful LAFF she has dat cums frum deep within her frame.

Yammo be there.

Solid. Me too. Make it bout 8pm-baby.

She blew me a Kiss thru da phone.

I returned the flavor.

And the countdown began to whut I felt was gittin retty to
be a SEMINAL moment in mo ways than one wit
Madame X.

I bizzied mah self with thawts of Mama cumming wile
making a kwik run to KRAZY DEALS STO owned by sum
good butt krazy old asians to grab a pint of her favorite pre-
packaged drank of APPLE MARTINI: heavy on the apple
cider/apple brandy/light on the Vodka.

Before I knew it-8pm was heah and Madame kalled me to
lemme kno she was on her way.

I peeped in mah Sanctuary and it saw it was all good and
retty to receive us for an episode of ritualistic cuppling &
counseling.

Seems like I had barely hung up and Madame was there.

It was a typickal sweltering/hot Summer in the city St Louis
NITE cuz the Sun had been acking a FOO all DAY.

She walked up into mah joint dressed in an expen-
sive/thin/long/chiffon see-thru dress dat showed off her
nutmeg-colored skin/lookin THICK as a TREE without da
Branches.

Sumpen bout mee U need to kno: a woman in a thin
long/see-thru dress make sumpen run thru mee down
deep.

And Madame X knows dat shit.

Wee hugged like lil kids doo when they bee happy 2 see

each otha when its been a minit: in other werds LONGS as a muthafucka.

Inside mah drawls mah Joint jumped to attention.

In the background mah Nigga DAVID RUFFIN was sangin n cryin bout LOST LOVING wile mee n Madame were bout to putt dat same loving on each otha--and make the nite even HOTTER.

In a way u cood say our Luv was un-requited.

U cood say dat butt it whudden be wholly true.

We segwayed down into The Sanctuary.

Mah hand was on her ample ass as she switched down the steps in front of me.

She was bout 2 tell me mo bout Abysinnia.

And I said: Hole dat thawt baby. Im strictly bout U and me rite now.

A few minutes lata wee were stripped nekkid n dancing up close n personal.

Wee boff broke out in dat SWEAT dat yo body recognizes when it knows sum lustful/black/sexual majick shit is bout 2 jump off.

31

Madame was def lookin good enuff to eat--and mah thawts were like Gumbo: a southern mixture of erry thang dat make-a-meal taste good in ya mouf when u swallow it.

Not to mention her smell.

She had on mah favorite scent.

HER!!

Madame always been natural wit it cuz she unnerstands the power of the bodys primal funky scent.

U may not katch mah meaning butt u needa kno dat when a woman go au naturel it heightens pheromones in a Man nose.

A Woman gotta do it jes rite tho.

Too long and she gone offend sumbody sense and sensibility in publick.

Butt done jes rite--its a Blessing n a Blissing to the rite muthafucka engaged in the realms of majick.

And 2nite I was the lucky Mayne bout to partake of a Womayne I have had a long addiction for dat I aint neva been able to shake--and truth be tole: I aint been wanting to shake it as mah Five SENSES were being Invaded by her ESSENCES.

Cuz at dat moment I strate realized dat erry thang I NEEDED was bout 2 bee SEEDED into mah Consciousness frum a woman I have neva been able to let go.

Sumpen else: Madame X is oh so SOFT. Soft to look at and soft to the Touch like cotton.

Her Nipples are the longest I have ever seen/surrounded by deep dark aureolas-dat when I kiss them they cum alive in mah mouf--and git even longer.

Her moan was gully n grimy as we fell into bed in a heated embrace/intertwined like one of St Louis famous Pretzels.

And as I nudged into her neck I thawt bout how she always warned me dat her NECK is one of her G-SPOTS--and how if I kiss her there--ITS ON LIKE NECKBONES!!

Butt now dat was Neck was unguarded.

I nestled in the crevice of its softness/raining gentle smooches frum top to bottom/katching her ear n shoulder blades too/all da parts of her dat needed attention.

And she is gently whispering thangs to me she reserves for our moments such as this.

I always want it 2 B like this Daddy.

I cood only mumble in agreement cuz i was lost in her powerful grip.

Then she whispered in mah ear: the mountains shall drop sweet wine and all the hills shall melt-baby.

I recognized the scripture immediately frum the soul skrolls.

It was of our favorites.

And I knew it was her sending me a thawt form that she was retty for me to show out between her bigg/brown gammish thighs.

Wee got into her favorite position: dat Missionary.

For a lotta folks the Missionary is old skool BUTT if U kno wut U doing its prolly the best to CLOWN n GIT DOWN In.

And da name cood not B mo appropriate for SACRED God Level fuckin fo MANIFESTATION.

Butt its always been dat deep/dark erotica way Madame has opened herself up to receive mah Membaship ya digg??

Madame leggs opened of their own free will/offering mee a look dat seemed like 2 mee i had not seen before.

The pussy was on fleek/wit a leak/gleaming/wet as water.

As I looked on I parted her lipps wit 2 fingaz in her hungry/yearning/wet honeypot.

I Spread n French Kissed her Labia Majora as they gave off an Aura--and wit mah fingaz still in her-let mah tongue play all up in the folds of her flower n amongst the multi-inches of bush hair surrounding her pit.

She began moanin sounds I had not heard before frum her.

I sucked her like a diabetik desperate for insulin/making gulping sounds as her lava flowed down mah throat--cuz imma freak dat way and im not satisfied if i dont BURP afta eating Pussy.

I felt her twitching as da Spirit of dat Thang ran thru her.

I continued being thoro n launched mah tongue as DEEP into her as I cood git it.

And she arched her back wit anutha animalistick moan to make it go even deeper.

Now I was in dat place in mah Mind I only go to when the Beast has risen frum the abyss of mah loins.

Its only Madam hoo kan make mee tap into dat zone.

As our mingled liquids/sweat rolled down between us-I putt mah hands underneath her ass and lifted her slitely/steady wit her clit in a tongue lock/simultaneously biting her thighs dat would have hickeys in 24 hours/nibbling the creases besides her pussy wit butterfly smooches.

Woooooooo!!!!

Madame let her soul cum out thru her mouf as she screamed like a banshee as the ORGASM took over her body.

I jes stayed bizzy.

I was dranking n eating her alive.

I wanted to have a LOVE HANGOVER afta we were done majickally manifesting.

She Busted anutha Orgasm all LOUD n shit--Squirmed in the sheets/turning this way n dat way.

Butt I kept her in mah grip cuz I was POSSESSED now.

While she was in the midst of cumming again she grabbed mah Rod and plunged it into her VAULT.

Thats what she called her Cookie: THE VAULT.

All 12 Inches of mah foot long disappeared inside Madame. I was on sum Big Dick Energy and she wanted it all.

She held me in a tite visegrip wit her thighs.

Needless to say I luv when Madame squeezes da fuck outta me wit her big ole thighs when Im dicking her down to the nth degree.

Butt 2nite was being/becumming even mo special 4 boff of us.

I was up to the HILT in Mama.

Butt I whudden thrusting yet.

I was jes laying in the Cut/mooving inside her wit Dick Perambulations (mo bout dat da next time we rap).

WAITING.

Then it happened:

She began speeking in the old/ancient language of tongues known as Kinaturu dat i spoke about previously in mah case wit Abysinnia.

I knew then she had gone into TRANCE and the SPELL of

Serious Fuckin was in affeck in a way it had never been befo wit us.

She was letting mee into a Place in DA PUSS EYE dat she had long ago STOPPED giving access to lousy muthafuckaz.

I caught her exotic werds dat urged me to navigate furtha within her to the portals dat only 2 lovers on one accord shood travel to in ecstasy 2getha.

Thats when I pinned her to the bed--and positioned mah feet in the Masonic Square known only to a few Niggaz such as mah self hoo are ensconced in the kinda werk i doo.

It was only then dat I began thrusting mah SNAKE slowly in and out of her Nest/her vaginal lipps quivering wit each n erry delicate stroke/she caressed the swollen vein dat ran da length of mah Shaft.

Madame has this thang she does wit her Pelvis dat oughta be patented.

Well-she did Dat Thang/timing mah erry plunge into the depths of her/allowing mee to hit that 2nd clit in the nether reaches of Da Pussy dat many-a-womayne doesnt even kno exists.

Wit erry Tap Madame NUTTED on mah Dick.

Im losing mah mind-Daddy!!!!

I said nothing.

I jes GROWLED wile her white juices ran down the length of mah organ as i pulled out for re-entry.

Dem spirits had arisen in me and brought da SAVAGERY wit it.

I kan take it-Daddy!!!!

Madame yelled: as she widened her leggs n grabbed her heels to allow the Dick up into her heart Chakra.

Feed Mee this muthafucka-guhl!! I growled it out.

She started shaking uncontrollably underneath me.

She cood not stop the tears frum flowing frum her eyes.

That caught me off guard a split second cuz in all of our past cupplings Madame had never cried--well--at lease NOT like this.

I knew den dat she was experiencing a form of SACRED HYSTERIA no womayne shood ever Sexperience--UNLESS she is giving dat thang up to the RITE muthafucka.

And this is where a lotta Wommin fuck up their Love Box-- and wind up becumming one of mah Clients.

Its krucial to overstand this.

Madame was cryin AND cumming at da same time--which brought down mah own shit.

I let up off the Gas and a NUT bogarted its way thru mah shaft and into da very Bak of Madame vault wit a Force I had not felt in a long time.

I saw stars like i had been punched in the temple as I Climaxed.

U see dem Stars-baby?? I whispered.

I see em too lova she answered.

We were holding each otha tite as hell as the last of power-ful/simultaneous orgasms rolled thru us.

I laid inside Madame for anutha 20 minutes afta we Busted 2getha cuz she liked dat feeling n da sound of me being STUCK inside her when i would PULL OUT.

We gradually parted and laid next to each otha wit da whole room smelling of fragrant fucking n love juices.

32

We were stunned/jes laying there in sticky silence.

We boff knew wee had gone sum place in our lovemaking/crossed boundaries n shit and Breathed LIFE into each otha.

Then rite on cue VOYAGE TO ATLANTIS by da ISLEY BROTHERS VOYAGE TO ATLANTIS song started playing frum the floor speekers.

Madame interrupted the quiet.

Daddy?

Yeah, Lova?

You kno how much I kare bout U rite?

Yeah. Mo den mah own Mama.

She smiled.

U werried bout sumpen tho?

Not exactly werried like scared or nuthing. Butt im koncerned dat this werk YOU doing. WE doing--is gonna attract the werst kinda enemies.

You mean like GREASY?

Yeah. Like GREASY lousy/oily ass.

We laffed--and I pulled her close 2 mee again.

Im serious tho-Daddy: We are affecting a lotta peeps 4 the good--and fools like Greasy dont like dat shit. The sexual vibrations of a lotta wommin were brought down low becuz of his no good ass. Not to mention dat sexual trafficking shit he connected to.

True. Butt Abysinnia case help putt a crip in his shit tho. THE ELDERS hoo run the metaphysikal circles are all ova his ass now too.

Really? I didnt kno it went up dat far?!

Um-Hm. It doo. On the downlow and jes between U/Mee and the bedpost--The Elders kontrol most of deez Spiritual Circles niggaz are in. Its kinda a secret unless u kno sumbody hoo KNO sumbody. Knowutimtombout??

I doo knowututombout-she said.

She rolled the werds 2getha da way I sed em cuz she always been in luv wit mah country way of talkin.

We jes started scratching the surface-Lova. Erry body hittin mee up.

I kno. And a lotta of werk will be cumming frum Sistaz I have passed on yo number too.

I figgered dat. BUTT jes so u kno I aint tryna do this shit without you guh!

You bet not even try-Daddy!!

Digg dat.

Butt PROMISE me sumpen-Lova Madame said.

Sho nuff. Wuts dat-Mama?

That we will always make time for each otha no matter wuts poppin off.

Shidddd-Imma make u MO den a Promise. Dats a GUARANTEE.

You kno I want you to help as many Wommin or Men as the case may be--as you kan. And I wanna help u doo it. Butt I dont want WE have to git lost in the mix-Daddy. I want wut we had n made here 2nite to be a Permanent thang between us.

Its automatic-baby. I NEED U like CORNFLAKES need MILK.

Like PEANUT BUTTER need JELLY?

Um-hm.

Like BACON need EGGS?

Allat. Like BREAF need STANK.

Aha-a-a-a-a-a!

We boff cracked up at our inside Jokes.

It was a moment being cherished.

And apparently one we didnt want to end.

33

Sumwhere between pillowtalking n joking wit Madame and
listening to the sounds of soul floating thru the room we fell
asleep all tangled up in each otha arms.

Thats why she called it the PRETZEL.

When I woke up the SUN was shining thru the window n
back showing its ass again.

Madame was up already cuz she gits up when dem god-dam
Birds start chirpin.

And since she kan burn in the kitchen like-a-muthafucka
She had alretty made me an old-fashioned/southern-stile
breakfast of skillet cornbread n gravy wit beef bacon and
extra Butter & pepper on the side. And a slice of watermelon wit salt.
Sidenote: If U dont eat yo eat watermelon wit salt Ion trust ya.

Why U putt dat loving on me like dat dere Mama?

*Shidddd-No YOU da one hoo clowned-Daddy. Ion kno wut u did butt
sumpen MAJOR happened last nite.*

No dout. Im lookin 4ward to mo of dat shit too.

Let da Chuch say amen. <a beat> Meanwhile-Lova-I need to git up and out and handle Nigga Bitness wit mah GIRLS.

I jes nodded in the affirmative.

I got outta da bed wit mah joint swangin n danglin da watusi.

Madame side-eyed it--then bent down n KISSED da Head.

You is Blessed-Daddy.

And highly favored.

Then: We hugged/kissed wit a warning frum me to her to watch out for mah Mornin Breaf. Which Madame ignored cuz she dont give-a-dam.

I walked her to the door.

We kissed again.

Miss Ya Til I Kiss Ya.

Miss Ya Til I kiss Ya she responded.

Then she was in the wind.

Back inside sublime thawts flooded mah mind.

Werd had rocketed round dat I had solved one of the most pressing cases of PUSSY DISAPPEARANCE the CONSCIOUS COMMUNITY had ever heard of.

And mah celly had been blowing da fuck up wit other Sistaz cumming forward wit stories of horrible deep hypocrisy about the LEADERS running these Metaphysikal Circles.

So the good news was dat da Pussy bizness was Booming.

The bad news was I whudden happy dat so many wommin were beeing taken advantage of in their quest for knowledge of their sexual self.

Howsumeva-this is cuz the werld is full of Un-Nice mutha-fuckin peeples wit ulterior/malevolent/e-vil spiritual motives. Yadigg?

Now if I had to doo this by mahself I would prolly be thinking twice.

Butt one thang I kno fo sho is dat Erry Body need SUM BODY when they are headed 4 wut cood be a DANGER ZONE.

Therefore I cood not THINK of ANY BODY I wanted mo 2 help mee serve this sexually konfused werld than The Indomitable/Inimitable WITCH Named MADAME X.

In shawt: I would be remiss and a CUMPLETE FOOL to leave her out of ANYTHANG dat Im involved in especially in da wise of DA PUSS EYE.

As I scarfed down wut she had lovingly prepared 4 mee da stark realization hit mee dat da Next Chapter of this werk I was dooing as REVEREND HOODOO DADDY: PUSSY DETECTIVE had really jes begun.

And I dont kno where it may end butt either way Madame X will be WIT me.

END

ACKNOWLEDGMENTS

I cant thank LEZA and CHRISTOPH of CLASH BOOK Fam enuff for this opportunity to show the world this vision of writing I have always had. They believed in what I have attempted with this genre of literature. And took a chance on me. They are what Indie Publishing should be.

ABOUT THE AUTHOR

I cum outta The South, by way of Louisiana and Tennessee. Life has Turned Me into A Savage Writer of Black Pulp Fiction, Black Exploitation, Black Folklore and Black Occult Erotica. Gritty Shit that makes You wanna Laff/Cry/Scream or Fuck.

RUMOR has it I was born from The last Nut in My Daddys Sack. And came into this world when HE came. Needless to say/My Birth was Traumatic. Thus, I arrived here with an Attitude. The Doctor Slapped Me and I Slapped Him Back. And So my Journey began. To Find Myself.

Contact me at: duvayknox@yahoo.com

ALSO BY CLASH BOOKS

DON'T PUSH THE BUTTON

John Skipp

LIFE OF THE PARTY

Tea Hacic

GIRL LIKE A BOMB

Autumn Christian

THE ELVIS MACHINE

Kim Vodicka

CHARCOAL

Garrett Cook

NO NAME ATKINS

Jerrod Schwarz

IF YOU DIED TOMORROW I WOULD EAT YOUR CORPSE

Wrath James White

SHITHEAD LAUREATE

Homeless

DIMENTIA

Russell Coy

JAH HILLS

Unathi Slasha

WE PUT THE LIT IN LITERARY

CLASHBOOKS.COM

FOLLOW US

TWITTER

IG

FB

PUBLICITY EMAIL

clashbookspublicity@gmail.com